Totally Bound Publishing books by Landra Graf

Bad Boys of Space
A Talent for Trouble
A Gamble Among Sheep
The Body Collector
A Mercenary to Love

I0663034

Bad Boys of Space

A MERCENARY TO LOVE

LANDRA GRAF

A Mercenary to Love
ISBN # 978-1-83943-998-8
©Copyright Landra Graf 2021
Cover Art by Erin Dameron-Hill ©Copyright July 2021
Interior text design by Claire Siemaszkiewicz
Totally Bound Publishing

Published in 2021 by Totally Bound Publishing, United Kingdom.

A MERCENARY TO LOVE

Dedication

To my bad boy with a heart of gold—this one's for you. And I didn't even muss my hair.

Chapter One

Whenever the planet Saturn had crossed Sampson's mind, he'd always believed stepping foot on its surface would involve jail time, or at the very least a spot in front of a tribunal. That he was being welcomed with open arms there, the land of the uppers, via official invitation no less, had made sleep near impossible for the last three solar days. Now, here he traveled among sprawling homes with green grass lawns, ponds of clear water...enough splendor to rattle the nerve endings of any man who'd grown up poor, near starving and covered in filth the majority of the time.

"Pull your mouth off the ground, kid. Bugs exist here." Lee, ex-assassin and weapon expert, whipped her long black ponytail over her shoulder as their holo-vehicle came to a stop in front of Ambassador Al Smith's house.

"You never told me how beautiful the ambassador planet was."

She scoffed and re-checked her belt that was normally stacked with knives lining the leather. Now only two remained. "The thing about beauty is that it comes with a price. No sense salivating over something you won't want to pay for."

Except, maybe I do.

Sampson had gone his whole life without much. Joining up with Smith's crew, back when the ambassador was a lowly body collector, Sampson had earned his place. When he'd ditched the Body Collection Service and joined the crew of *Gina*, he'd found a family. Regardless of the gains, there still existed this gnawing need inside him for more.

"You could have something like this, bet on it. Show these pansy fools your big brain in action." Lee nudged him on the shoulder before she hopped out of the vehicle. "Enough sitting around talking. Let's do this."

Sure, he probably could reach living on Saturn status. Al had. The captain of a death barge was now a parliament ambassador, a fairy-tale story like the ones his mother used to spout over their dinner of broth and stale food cubes. The possibility of living on a wealthy planet in a fancy house tempted, but he wanted another kind of freedom. Living here would only be another prison of servitude. The desire to roam space, go where he wanted when he wanted, to eat what he wanted... All those wants drove him on.

"Welcome to my home," Al called out from the front door, all fancy robes, ginger beard tamed and his infamous nose ring a thing of the past.

Sampson gave a single nod out of respect and instinctually reached to tug on the edge of the beanie he typically wore on the ship. "Thanks for the invite."

"Would you like a tour?" The older man's booming voice carried across the lawn with ease.

Sampson patted down his ginger hair and glanced at Lee, whose raised eyebrow told him everything he needed to know. "Perhaps another time. This is supposed to be a business trip, and I'd like to get to work right away."

The words rolled off Sampson's tongue like contaminated waste in a slip drive, foreign and unwelcome. He wanted to throw caution to the wind, take a tour or enjoy a fancy lunch—which was exactly why Lee had come along, to keep him focused.

The invitation from Al had come in a solar week before and Gina, the ship's artificial intelligence, had been eager to share with Sampson how his expertise was requested along with the possible payday involved.

Enough crinkle to bathe in, according to Gina. Their co-captains, Toni and Emilio, were busy with another gig and had graciously offered up *Gina* along with the remainder of the crew to escort him. *More like babysit.* The implication stung a bit but made sense. *Gina* wasn't a cheap ship, and she'd been hijacked before. Though if he completed this job, the flash was his for the taking, and maybe...

I'll have enough to buy Gina.

"Straighten up, kid. Don't let yourself be intimidated by him. You're smarter." Lee casually whispered these words on their walk up.

The encouragement soothed his shaken soul a bit. The last time he'd encountered Al Smith, Sampson had been indentured to Al's body collection barge with a twenty-year service tag. Al hadn't been horrible to work for, but he'd still been in charge and not afraid to stow a young boy in a small crappy room in the underbelly of the ship.

Sampson and Lee reached the front entrance, and he took note of the pair of guards posted right inside. *Business trip indeed.*

"Yes, and once you get inside, we can chat. You don't mind if the guards search you?" Al asked with a sheepish smile.

Trust doesn't come easy anywhere in this damn galaxy. They'd been searched three times since they'd gotten off *Gina*'s shuttle at the landing port. *No such thing as a small measure for the planet housing parliament's ambassadors.*

Lee smiled, a wicked fucking grin equal parts 'screw you' and 'sure thing.' "Do what you have to, but my knives stay. I already put away half of them. The rest is for your protection and Sampson's. Anything happens to him, and you'll be answering to your sister personally if I don't get you first."

Pride swelled in Sampson's chest. *Family.* These people cared about him, though sometimes he wished they would let him run his own missions. *Let me take charge.* Sure, he'd been told he was in charge on this one by Emilio, but Lee still played the role of big bad sister no matter what.

Al held up his hands. "Sure thing. Just making sure no explosives and whatnot. Loyda would be pissed if I didn't follow protocol."

Sampson nodded in agreement, standing up straight and spreading his arms. "Then let's wrap this and get to it. Time is flash."

* * * *

One week later

"Will it be all right for us to play outside once this goes live?" the nanny of the household asked as she swayed gently back and forth. She'd been shy and quiet at first, but within the first three days, she had come around whenever Sampson was working, asking questions, talking about his smarts. Normally, he'd be flattered by the attention, but duty called.

"Yes, once the system is live, you'll be able to go anywhere on the Smiths' property with Jace and still be safe." He grabbed another gauge reader from his belt to measure the voltage coming from the box. Everything needed to be perfect.

The nanny, a petite brunette named Bridget, let out a little giggle as she pressed a hand against her upper chest. "Oh, such a relief. You have no idea how much this will make getting fresh air less of an ordeal. It's been months since Jace enjoyed a good outside picnic, what with all the threats."

A thread of anger weaved through Sampson like a current coursing through wire. No child should have his life threatened, especially when the kid had no choice over who his parents were or where he came from. Sampson empathized with the need to keep the kid safe, one of the reasons he'd accepted the damn job.

"Well, hopefully, this will keep everyone in the house safe. Now, Nanny—"

"Yes?" She reached out and rested her pale hand against his forearm. Nothing came with the connection, no sparks, no desire.

Damn. She had a cute smile, a pleasant demeanor…everything he should have wanted in a woman.

"Nanny Bridget, I have to finalize a few things while we wait for the APU approval on the designs to come through. I want to make sure everything is ready to go live as soon as we get the say-so." Sampson glanced meaningfully at the door.

The nanny gasped as understanding finally hit. "Yes, and I am in the way. I'll just get back to Master Jace. He'll probably be up from his nap any minute."

She left, and Sampson was grateful to be alone again. Sure, he liked a pretty face, but she offered little else. Besides, the project called to him. There was something about computers, electricity, ships, engines, software, hardware...it didn't matter the technology involved when it sang to Sampson, like a melody he could memorize. He had to take things apart, put them back together or build something new entirely.

He'd been damn good at disassembly and found new purpose in fixing broken things only to make them better and more interesting than they'd been in the first place. This new security system he'd built for Al and his wife, Loyda, was no exception. State of the art with thermal imaging, body scanning, pressure sensors that gauged each member of the family, staff, and security—anything the slightest bit off, and it would trigger a full-scale alert.

Of course, Al hadn't been lying about the Allied Planetary Union investigation division wanting details. They had requested the full schematics before the system could go live and demanded the right to change anything they saw fit.

More like steal my shit.

Exactly why he didn't give them everything, but only enough to satisfy them with the false belief they'd seen all he offered. Lee had given him the same advice years ago. "*Never tell people what you are fully capable of or they'll try to control you or kill you.*"

Jealousy and the desire to possess power—those were the things Sampson had encountered time and again. He focused on the control panel set up in the Smiths' office. He checked each circuit and wire with the gauge in his hand, reading the electricity currents coursing through them. The system had to be perfect or —

"Almost done in here?"

A spark arced as Sampson jerked at Lee's words. *Fatch.* "Lee, could you save the sneaking-up crap for Al's hired guns?"

She grinned and walked forward. "Those aren't hired guns. More like hired targets. Saw that nanny come flying out of here. Almost swore there were tears in her eyes from you sending her away."

"Yeah, better tears than hearts. Can't say we would work out."

Lee clucked. "Now, Sampson. Just because one woman did a number on you doesn't mean we're all bad."

One woman…*the* woman. Zasha had been all that mattered, had made him burn brighter than a ship slip drive at full power. *Then* — "I get plenty of action without getting deep and meaningful."

He'd wanted the full romance bit once.

"It may be worth giving it a shot again. Besides, the nanny isn't bad-looking."

Sampson shook his head and swiped the mess of hair out of his face. "You were right when we arrived. No sense going after something I don't want to pay the price for."

Not after the last time.

Sampson thrust a gauge meter towards Lee. "Instead of standing around trying to scare people, I could use your help with the last security checks."

"Fine, but after this we go for a drink?"

"Sure." Sampson released the tool to her and went back to his work, not looking forward to a drink at all.

* * * *

Zasha Gustaf stared at the communiqué in front of her. The directive had come in overnight, but the words didn't make sense.

Evaluate the home of Ambassador Smith and ensure it's safe.

They'd been sent to Saturn to gain intel from parliament contacts and weapon supplies to take back to Earth's moon. Not to engage in clandestine spying on a planet more heavily guarded by the law than any other place in the universe.

Her days of subterfuge, killing and fucking to forget were over. At least that had been the plan when she'd ditched the Mercenary Guild and joined up with the Humans First Movement. The group was all about stopping the exploitation of human flesh and bone to power engines by the APU—by anyone. She believed there was a better way and supported the effort to save and enrich lives instead of snuffing them.

Kascade Harbinger, the leader of Humans First, had made her believe in a positive, humanity-first future.

Exactly why he might be trying to get this meeting going with Al Smith.

The infamous body collector, now an ambassador, had recently announced a push in parliament to approve adding the lower planets, Mars, Earth's moon and Earth as official members. This would give them representation, a chance to have ambassadors speak as the voice of the people. Though Kascade had never implied he wanted a spot in parliament, he did mention in his speeches to the group how he wanted those in the uppers to see the damage and destruction their current mode of space travel caused.

"We could walk right up to the door." She handed the communiqué over to Darren, a tall, medium-built guy who operated as one of Kascade's right hands. Zasha sat lower on the authority ring, but since Kascade had sent her here, she had to be valuable. She had a skill for anticipation and suspicion, which had come from her previous trade. Though, with all this sneaking around, her tingle of concern had dialed up a few notches.

Did Kascade have other plans for people like her? She wasn't the only ex-merc attracted to the movement. There were plenty of them tired of taking lives, but perfectly capable if a need arose.

Think positive, think light, believe trust.

She fell back on the motto they spoke at the end of every gathering. Her chance to make a difference started here. *With trust.* Living a life of ulterior motives and clandestine plans lay behind her.

Darren frowned, his forehead collapsing into a network of wrinkles as he read over the holo-sheet in his hands. "He wants this to be done quietly. Walking up is no option."

No joke, spacehole.

Darren had his pants cinched too tight. The guy, with his near-black eyes and perpetually stoic nature, who towered over her when standing upright, had lost his sense of humor out in space somewhere. He couldn't catch a suggestion or a joke if it sucked his ass into a black hole.

"I get that, which is why I said that sarcastically."

"We follow the directions to the note. No deviation."

"Right, because we're not supposed to be here."

Where the hell did Kascade get this guy? Why does he trust him?

Sure, almost every member of Humans First came from some sort of dubious background. Most of them had failed to lead a wealthy life, and legitimate employment that kept food on the table was hard to come by. That they were in a small-ass room with two cots, a table and two chairs, hidden above a grocery shop, only added to the aesthetic. No way would they have been welcomed with open arms by APU forces on this planet. They had ridden in on a supply vessel, holed up among produce and crackers, with little buttons attached to their shirts to fool sensors.

If I never smell a cracker again, it will be too soon.

Zasha longed for a good slice of beef, even an egg. But crackers, crappy food cubes and the occasional grape or apple were all the shopkeeper dared to send up to ensure no one suspected he gave food away.

"Are you ready to go?" Darren asked.

"Let me grab my scanner." *And a knife.* Hell, she'd let paranoia in again, fears of being double-crossed, used and left for dead. *Not the place.*

Especially when she needed to focus on the main point, completing the job and earning another notch of respect in this surrogate family. She wanted to be involved in the big plans and, like in any organization, rising to the top came with missions, efforts and a whole lot of red tape.

But no more cheating my way there by physically knocking out the competition.

Darren opened the hatch in the floor, flooding their small hiding space with natural light from the room below. They climbed down from the rafters, one after the other. The sun was mid-day, the way it remained for half a solar year on Saturn. The majority of residents got their windows screened, designed to reflect a similar twenty-four day like Earth. *Nothing like the pleasure moon, Callisto, with its satellite sun-screens.* No, these rich folks of the uppers enjoyed living whole months in sunlight followed by total darkness.

Darren didn't say much to the shopkeeper, simply gave a nod and walked out of the front door.

Zasha shrugged at the older man, who thankfully didn't have any customers. "Sorry, he lacks some social graces."

"It's fine. Whatever is needed for the movement. Just remember to be back in before the midnight gong. Otherwise, you could be brought in for questioning."

Zasha nodded and tugged at the hem of her knee-length tunic while adjusting the scanner she'd tucked into her belt. She felt as awkward as a mercenary in a church, wearing these Saturn-style clothes the shopkeeper had given them. Her standard getup, designed more for space travel, was stashed above in their room. They had to fit in, which was why Zasha's tri-colored hair was down and flowing around her shoulders, instead of up in the twin buns she usually wore.

Focus on the mission.

She walked out through the shop door and jogged to catch up to Darren. "Don't leave me behind."

"Then keep up."

Zasha wished Kascade's other right hand had been assigned on this adventure. At least *she* could hold a conversation. But no, Tia remained at their base on the Earth's moon.

The added element to their mission bordered on ridiculous, and unnecessary. Did Kascade want to meet with Ambassador Smith? Sure, the big bill in parliament would allow the lower planets more say in government, giving Humans First a chance to speak their opinions to the ruling factions with ease and forward the cause.

"Is there going to be a meeting between the boss and Smith? Or is the boss worried someone might attack him?" If Smith were removed, the efforts for the lowers would be blown.

Darren grunted. "Not for me to know or you to worry about."

More non-answers. She wasn't nosy as a rule, but she enjoyed having knowledge of the possibilities for…reasons. Her old mentor had always said reasons were her problem, as pesky as morals and ethics. Except she'd seen enough death to make knowledge matter and inside information always helped her determine her exit strategy.

The lack of response from the double jerk beside her only elevated her wariness. Maybe they had a plan. Maybe Kascade wanted to fight for more rights, more technology and less stealing. Moon tech remained in constant demand by those in the uppers in exchange for things like food and medical supplies.

Things the Moonies should receive without a cost tag attached.

Food and medical care were supposed to be basic human rights.

Her musing got her through the walk, as they trudged past fancy houses on brick sidewalks lining paved roads. No dusty dirt-carved crevices from holo-bikes and racers or trash litter, and no huddles of children or women peddling their bodies seeking enough crinkle to get them through another day.

Serious fancy and oh, so fake.

Then she came to a halt in front of something far more impressive, a long winding drive guarded by an entrance gate. Bushes and shrubs lined the pavers leading up to a two-story house of glass and steel, all of it tinted with the latest technology could offer. Square doors. Bright green, with gilded gold trim glinting against the sunlight. A sparkling roof designed to absorb every bit of energy, converted to power the home.

If we can solar-power buildings, why not ships?

Darren headed off the main road as if he wanted to inspect the rose bushes. Gardener he was not, but the efforts did the trick and the two guards at the gate only gave them a cursory glance.

"Come, sister. Look at these roses."

She trotted over and pulled out her scanner. To the cursory glance, her handheld tech could be anything. The scanner was her own personal design, improved on over the years, and could pick up people, calculate hiding spots, places for possible ambush, hiding passages and security systems.

"Looks like the Smiths are getting an upgrade."

Darren leaned down as he fondled a rose with one hand and cast a shadow over her. "What kind of upgrades?"

"Hard to tell since the system isn't online yet, but connections are being upgraded with copper-infused wiring, and there's a separate switch box in the office, meaning the security will be separate from the rest of the house. If you take out the main power, you won't take this out. Smart."

Only one person was capable of such a thing, and Zasha's heart thumped at the possibility of her red-haired tech genius being so close to her. Though technological brains were fast becoming a flash a dozen, based on the big ideas she caught wind of from hanging out with the people on the moon.

As if conjured from her memory, a bite-sized red-headed version of the man on her mind came racing across the wide expanse of green yard. He wore a maroon tunic with black sandals and had blue eyes...not green.

Zasha took a few steps forward, caught up in the innocence of the little boy with a carefree smile and no trace of fear or betrayal in his face.

This can't be Sampson's.

"Hey, where's Lee?" A smoky male voice wrapped itself around Zasha and sent her hurtling over eight years into her past. Her eyes closed as she let the deep, silvery tones throw her back to pleasant moments. She'd loved Sampson's lilt. The timbre embodied warmth amid darkness and acted like a cocoon of blankets.

Opening her eyes, Zasha saw the object of her dreams and regrets standing yards away, walking out through the front door of the Smiths' house. She kept scanning and slowly, deliberately made her way towards the gate and the guards on duty. Darren appeared to be working separate reconnaissance, oblivious to her, until the alarm went off.

Zasha hunched over and dived into the nearest bush. "Darren," she whispered.

He glanced over at her and followed her lead as the buzzing noise around the front gates increased in volume.

"We need to go." She popped out the memory chip in the scanner and shoved it toward him. "Take this information and send it on. If Kascade is planning to meet Al here, there'll be plenty of security within the next twenty-four solar hours."

"How many people?" Darren asked, but Zasha shushed him as she heard Sampson start talking.

"We need to finish the upload and get the rest of these sensors placed and this time, don't trigger them." Sampson's voice rang out loud and clear as the droning alarms turned off. sounding far more authoritative than when she'd known him. The boy with the red hair had lost some of his sweetness.

Unfortunate. And unsurprising, after what I did.

Darren nudged her and almost made her fall backward. "How many?"

Zasha grabbed for the bush branches in front of her to steady herself, then glanced at the screen. "I scanned four guards, a child and his caretaker, plus these other two working on the system. Don't have the Smiths here — at least it's not picking up their bio scans."

"Then we go. Report to Kascade." Darren grabbed the chip before he poked his head out. Whatever he saw didn't faze him, because the fool stood right up and started strolling back the way they'd come.

Zasha stopped short of rolling her eyes and pushed herself out of the bushes, tucking her scanner into her belt underneath the tunic. One last glance at the front door and Sampson looked her way. She whirled around quickly. There was a lot that they needed to say to each other, and even more that she needed to apologize for.

Except, the time for their reunion hadn't arrived yet.

Seeking redemption can be a bitch.

Chapter Two

"Here's to another day's work finished." Lee hoisted a glass of clear liquid and clinked it against Sampson's. She downed it, slammed it on the table then nudged his boot with hers. "What the hell is the problem this time?"

Sampson didn't want to answer. They'd wrapped for the day, and Lee had demanded he leave with her to get a drink because she "*wouldn't be judged for getting into Al's liquor cabinet.*" Too much bad blood still remained between the two.

It was a long story spanning back more than eight years, when Toni, Al's sister, had separated herself, Lee, Sampson and a couple of others from Al's crew. Times Sampson didn't think about because they brought back the memories of…her.

He rubbed a hand over his face and stared at the glass of liquor.

She was there. No, I'm seeing shit again.

"Nothing. Ready to be done." He picked up the glass fully intending to drink the swill inside but held off.

So here they sat, in some market part of town, in a bar with low lighting and suffering with a two-drink maximum because government powers didn't want anyone to get wasted. A silly rule since the bottles were so heavily watered down no one could get the slightest buzz. If Sampson wanted a real drink, he'd have to go back to *Gina*, who sat in orbit.

The ship hadn't checked in for more than a day and only had Doc and Dottie for company. He imagined the AI was lonely, the same way he longed for adventure and more than ransack jobs. A chance to travel the stars, without ties.

Sampson twisted his glass against the wood tabletop. "Ready to get this done, get paid and return to *Gina*."

The security system sat ready, all sensors in place, wires secured, cameras angled and thermals ready to activate. His most ambitious project yet, completed and undeployed because of bureaucratic bullshit, when he'd prefer to be back with his best friend and in his own bed.

Plus, a chance to take the next step in my plan.

Lee lifted her hand, signaling to someone she wanted another drink. "This wouldn't have something to do with your wacky idea about buying *Gina* and breaking our family up?"

Her statement got him sitting up straight, gripping his glass a little too tight, enough so the fancy fake booze sloshed out a bit onto his hand. "How did you know about that?"

"I wouldn't wait too long. Emilio and Toni won't like being blindsided."

If Lee had discerned his plans, then both Emilio and Toni had too.

Shit.

This was what he wanted to prevent. They'd given him a family! When his mother and father had sold him off to indentured servitude with the BCS at the earliest chance, because he hadn't possessed any type of talent they needed, he'd vowed never to be in a situation so depressing again. *Thrown away for crinkle.* Emilio and Toni valued him, and at least he'd proved useful to their enterprise.

"It's not about wanting to break the crew up. I'm looking for a chance to break out on my own. To make decisions for me, like a grown-up."

Lee lifted one eyebrow and pulled one of her knives out from her vest. "Grown-up? Seems to me taking a job while Toni and Emilio are finishing up a separate one is pretty grown-up. Besides, you don't need *Gina* to act on your own."

Yes, I do.

Gina might have been a ship, but the AI within had evolved beyond a simple computer processor in space. She'd become his best friend. He told her everything and vice versa. They'd spent the last eight years together. During those endless hours spent in space, he'd become closer to her than almost anyone else. Besides, who would help her grow if he left? She had feelings too and she needed him.

"Lee, we're a pair. We go together."

"Pfft. Yeah," Lee's drink showed up, and the lady who dropped it off winked at her. The simple flirtation was enough to get Lee's attention. "You say that because you don't bother to get close to anyone flesh and blood. You can't let—"

"Don't say her name, please." Sampson downed the imitation vodka with the poor weak burn, which only made him crave the real stuff.

She was there today.

"You can't run from the past." Lee's words were half-hearted, her focus drawn to the roaming waitress.

"Says the woman who never talks about hers." His accusation got the assassin's gaze on him.

"There's a difference between running and talking. I've faced all my demons and won. I don't need to re-hash something with no hold or sway over me. You, on the other hand, get all clammed up at the mere mention of someone who hurt you. You confront those things, or they eat you up inside. This I can speak of with authority."

Lee pushed her seat back and stood. Sampson sat in awe of this woman's confident nature, in full possession of every part of herself. He wanted to be the same. To know himself as well as Lee did. To be settled in his skin.

"Now, if you'll excuse me. The woman who brought our drinks is fatching me with her eyes, and I intend to do something about it. Don't wait around for me. Head back to Al's whenever."

Every port we stop in. Sampson grinned. "Have a good time."

"Oh, I will."

Lee winked. With her half-empty vest of knives and swaying ponytail, she moved away without a sound.

Sampson glanced at his glass. It sat empty, like the deepest parts of him. Not an unfamiliar experience as Sampson found himself included by the other members of the crew, but still treated as a kid. Sure, they cared about him, but eager for him to tag along or spend time outside of missions with him not so much. He found himself lonely more often than not, and wishing he had a closer friend, someone more his age.

"Hello, Sampson. Long time."

His gaze traveled from his glass to the woman who'd propped one knee on the chair Lee had abandoned. Red-brown-blonde hair was down and flowing freely instead of wrapped up in the woman's usual twin buns, and an odd-colored tunic of the Saturn style hung past her waist but accented her creamy tan skin and gold eyes. This new look, paired with her stance, made her seem more innocent.

But I know better.

Between his blood pounding, the remembrance of her cries of pleasure and the explosive concussion and her betrayal, sounds flooded his ears. She'd stolen from him, his crew. He'd fallen so hard, young, dumb...thinking with his swinging pipe.

Zasha. She was *there today.*

She'd betrayed them when they'd helped her. Lied to him, his family...for flash.

Sampson fisted the empty glass so tightly it cracked. "Not long enough."

* * * *

Zasha should have stayed in the shop, but she'd begged off from Darren's company after he'd uploaded the scanner data. She'd left the report filing to Darren as her insides hummed with anxious energy and had taken up a perch on a flat-topped building next door to the store. A precautionary countermeasure, she'd told Darren.

He'd given a grunt of approval. The idiot only cared about his precious report.

Sure enough, her instincts had proved right. Lee and Sampson had come into the market mere hours after they were at the Smiths'. Of course, she'd figured Lee would already be aware of her presence, but the other woman had made no attempt to track her. Interesting.

Zasha should have reported her findings to Darren and given him a warning. No more screwing around, taking chances—they should depart immediately, but the deep-seated desire for redemption wedged a nail into her normal duty-bound manners.

Sampson.

The one she'd fallen for, who sat in this crappy excuse for a bar, all grown up, but still with a distant, wistful, dreaming face. They'd talked for solar hours about what they would do if flash weren't an issue, if the APU had no control over their lives and if food and water came without a cost.

Then she'd done what Sampson hated the most— lied and betrayed him.

His fallen smile and hunched eyebrows at her arrival weren't surprising. She should have waited to approach him, but...when would she have the chance? If his crew still operated the same way, once the job wrapped up, he would be gone.

She had one shot.

Zasha set a pair of drinks on the table. "I understand why you would say that. I wasn't exactly the best person back then, but I'm trying to be better. Exactly why I want to talk to you."

Sampson unclenched his grip on the glass. His red hair had gotten long, his usual beanie nowhere in sight. She missed the cap he used to wear over his head. His eyes weren't on her, and a part of her deeply longed for a stare from those soulful green depths.

"You say the words 'better person,' yet you're here in Saturn garb. I don't see a ring on your finger, so who are you sneaking on-world to assassinate this time?

Must be a lot of crinkle up for grabs to draw your attention."

The words were filled with vitriol, but she didn't let them bother her. Hurt and anger festering over many years could eat away at one's soul. She'd been the same way once.

Yet, you still doubt everything.

"No, this isn't a bad situation or a crinkle one." She slid into the booth and pulled up the sleeve of her tunic to show the tattoo. Her next words were delivered in a whisper. "I'm with Humans First."

She put the sleeve back in place as quickly as she could. *No sense in drawing any more attention.* They weren't being loud, but Sampson's hunched shoulders and permanent scowl failed to help their situation if anyone paid close attention.

Sampson scoffed. "You traded one morally reprehensible group for another—why am I not surprised?"

"This group isn't like the last one. I'm not a merc anymore. No more killing for flash. I signed up to save lives."

Sampson reached for one of the glasses and let out a small sigh. "Fine. Whatever you have to say, I'll give you until I finish this crappy swill to do it."

Zasha took a deep breath, the Humans First chant silently rolling in her brain. She could take only so much negative attitude directed at her. "Regardless of why I am on Saturn, I am trying to make amends to those I've hurt. You are at the top of the list. I don't expect immediate forgiveness but I wanted to tell you I'm sorry nonetheless."

Sampson rolled his eyes and picked up the glass. "I'll be done in a second."

Zasha clenched her fists. "What happened to civility, at least? The Sampson I remember gave everyone a moment to have their say."

He slammed the empty glass onto the tabletop, cracking it similarly to the one he'd held in his hand when she approached. "Get spaced."

Zasha stared at him some more, and finally he gazed back. Those green eyes were hardened with anger, something she'd seen plenty in the mercenary guild when she'd roamed its ranks. "Fine. But I hope one day..."

The words were pointless. She slid from the chair and walked out of the bar without looking at him one more time.

The sounds, sights, even the ever-present sun were blobs of nothing. It was funny how this lack of connection to the one person she'd shared so much of her true self with hurt. She wanted him more than ever.

You don't deserve him.

The past assailed her as she made her way down the market street to the shop where her rooms waited. How she'd almost died and Sampson, along with Gina, had found her flaming ship. Sampson had vouched for her when the rest of his crew would have left her for dead. They'd immediately connected, bonding over a love of technology.

Over the course of two weeks traveling toward Io, they'd become inseparable...partially because Emilio and Toni wouldn't let her move about on her own. They'd been right not to trust her.

Still, it didn't stop her and Sampson from joining in the most primal of ways. She tugged at the collar of her tunic as her skin flushed with heat. He'd given her the best of him...she'd been his first.

You're a piece of work, Zasha.

She reached the store, and inside, the shopkeeper assisted a male couple. So, she wandered, unable to go up to her room until they left. This was what Sampson railed against, subterfuge. He would consider her sneaking around horrible and dishonest.

I've done worse.

She'd done whatever needed to get the flash. To line her pockets so she wouldn't starve or suffer like her brother had.

"Feelings won't keep a belly full" her mother had repeated every night, like some sort of prayer designed to teach Zasha to be ruthless. Her mercenary mentor, Jennifer, had attempted to reinforce those corrupt morals, but ruthless meant forever alone and often included people suffering needlessly.

The door chimed, signaling the customers were gone.

"Take this upstairs with you, Zasha." The shopkeeper motioned her over to the main counter and pointed to a basket. "Some dinner for you both. May the movement thrive."

"Hopefully, with this and our report we have for today, we shall. Thank you for your kindness and may we get our orders to depart soon."

The shopkeeper inclined his head but offered no response. *A man of few words.* Though again, Darren and Kascade repeatedly encouraged her to refrain from asking questions or pestering people for extra conversation. Often, members of Humans First could only do what they did in anonymity and to dig deeper violated the support they gave to the movement.

She hoisted the basket in one hand before climbing up the ladder. Once there, the ceiling hatch shut and secure, she opened the basket.

"What's that?" Darren asked after a quick glance in her direction. The majority of his focus was on a holo-vid screen in front of him.

"Food. Want some?"

She hated offering because Darren became a bottomless pit around food. He'd eat everything in sight. She grabbed an apple and a few food cubes. Her encounter with Sampson hadn't left her with much of an appetite. Hell, she'd left her drink.

"Did the report go through?"

Darren grunted as he stuffed food cubes into his mouth.

"When will we get a response?"

Darren gave a shrug and turned back to his holo-vid screen. "Kascade will let us know the next steps in his own time."

Zasha wasn't sure what held his attention, and she didn't care, deserving at least a couple of hours to wallow in her failure. She climbed onto her cot, finished her food, then lay down. Being in Humans First meant she didn't need to watch out for herself every five minutes or worry about a double-cross. People cared for one other.

Falling asleep was near impossible now, with the look in Sampson's angry eyes stamped on her brain like a brand.

Chapter Three

Sampson finished Zasha's abandoned drink just as Lee came back.

"Do we need to alert the authorities?"

Hell. The last thing any of them needed was more attention. Zasha, for all her machinations and messes, could dig her own holes and a way out of them.

"Leave her be."

Lee frowned. "This from the very person with his heart all torn up and shit? I glanced over to check on you before heading out and I'm glad I did. Besides, if she's here, there's trouble brewing."

"By tomorrow morning, it won't be our problem." Sampson refused to care, because if he did, then he'd try to find her.

"Fine. I'll go back to my good time. Maybe you should get some rest, too."

Rest? He'd get plenty once the job wrapped and he got off this damn planet. "Sure. Don't stay too long. Implementation is happening as soon as the approval comes through." He shoved himself out of the chair and left the bar.

But each step away from the would-be-fancy swill hole only made him hate himself more, as he did the very thing he'd willed himself not to. He searched for her, eyes roving over every street merchant and corner shop. She wasn't what he'd come to Saturn for, but when it came to Zasha—knowing she still breathed air…

Fatch.

Once upon a time, Sampson had planned on being with her, having her along for the ride with him and Gina. They could have spent the last eight years on adventures together, not apart and separately fighting their own paths. Broody as hell, he stomped his way back toward the Smiths' house, the wound she'd left him with the first time exploding open, as if newly inflicted.

Never healed, never fully mended. Lee's words haunted him too about prices to pay, about wants and needs. His heart being torn open.

He needed his friend now more than ever. While Lee offered little gems from time to time, Gina kept him grounded. She got him, understood the type of person he was and what he sought.

He would never be free of Zasha as long as he and Gina continued to operate under Emilio and Toni's banner. They needed to break out on their own, make their own way and escape these dead-end jobs. Sampson needed to meet someone else, someone who cared more about him than flash or a cause. Zasha always had her causes.

He should have discussed things more with Lee before he'd left. Deep down, he dismissed Zasha's appearance, but Emilio always said there was no such thing as coincidence. Typically, if something happened it meant a reason. It meant *pay attention.*

Frustration gripped him anew. *Why now?* Of all the places, and times, he could have run into this woman, why did she pop up right when he was about to get his shit in order?

A curse rested on him for sure, with things inside his sphere of living always getting cocked up. The crew would be on the path to success and some wrench would arrive to loosen the screws. *Right on time.*

He made his way down the winding drive toward Al's home. The guards at the door let him pass, and he stumbled into the main room, the scene before him too domestic, sweet and with more family emotion than he'd ever have.

Al and Loyda sat on the floor with their young son, Jace, as the boy toddled on unsure feet between them.

Gasps of delight echoed through the room as Jace traversed the short distance. Sampson clapped to be polite and to alert them to his presence.

"Ah." Al glanced up from his son in his arms. "You've returned. Where's your shadow?"

"Lee stayed in town, found a friend."

Al nodded. "Of course. She always does. We are still waiting on approval, but I'm told I'll have it before bedtime."

"Sounds good."

Jace made a noise, and Al's focus went back to the boy who was now building something out of hand-sized blocks. Ever-attentive parents, Al and Loyda participated with their son.

Loyda spoke without looking at Sampson. "Dinner is done, but we have some food put away for you in the kitchen…if you want it."

She played the role of hostess well, a surprise since he'd met her prior to her taking over her duties as an ambassador. She'd been an APU investigator, hunting down those who committed crimes against the government, which had led her to Al and another love story… *Something I'll never have.*

"Appreciate the offer. I might grab something in a bit, but first I need to check in with Gina."

He left before either of them could speak again, letting their attention remain on their child. What he wouldn't have given to have parents half as doting, as caring. He'd only received attention when he proved useful—in actions, not words. *Words are a waste.*

He got into his room, grabbed his vid-screen and typed in the encrypted codes. *Trust no one.* That had become his mantra since the Zasha episode. He needed to talk with Gina.

"Hello, Sampson." Her voice came in crystal clear, yet monotone. He could still pick up the tiny alterations implying that she was happy to chat.

"Gina, how are things in orbit?"

She changed the screen to show him the outside of the ship. "We have only one APU cruiser watching us now. The other has been deployed elsewhere. They conduct a scan every thirty minutes."

"Are the defensive measures we put in place working?"

"Yes, they see only what we want them to. Still feels a little like I have a peeping tomb."

For all her upgrades and integration of old Earth knowledge, languages and syntax, she still mixed words and metaphors. Sampson chuckled. "It's a peeping Tom, not a tomb."

"Yes, either way. When are you done? I have been keeping close watch and your project is complete."

Of course she would turn her cameras planet-side.

"As soon as parliament approves the design."

"Will this give us enough?" Gina had always been fully involved with his plan to buy her from Emilio and Toni. He could never have kept it from her because she would have rebelled in a heartbeat if forced into something against her will.

"I believe it might. There's a lot of flash on the table. Almost as much as those jobs the crew did for Sweet years ago. Speaking of, you'll never guess who I—"

"Sampson." His name was coupled with a brief knock then Al stuck his head through the open crack in the door. "We have the approval."

"Gotta go, Gina."

"Good luck."

Sampson shut down the holo-vid connection and put the screen away. "Then by all means, let's get started on the implementation."

They walked into Al's office where Loyda waited and Jace was nowhere to be seen.

"How complicated is this?" Al asked as they reached the control box.

Sampson shrugged. "Not very. We have to flip a switch and within fifteen seconds, the system will take control. After that you'll have similar technology to what Gina is capable of, but without the speaking AI."

He opened the cover of the box, excitement coursing through his veins, as it did any time he activated a completed project. This is what he'd been waiting for. *What I need after this shitty evening. A win.*

He reached for the switch, ready to flip it, then the lights went out. The house let out a collective hum as everything powered down. Glass shattered and Sampson froze in position. A second passed before he caught up with the disaster unfolding. Everything he'd been working for messed up and destroyed. *Shit!*

Jabbing at the communication device on his wrist, he remote-connected to Gina, audio-only. "Gina, plug into the house. Don't care if the APU detects you. Do it quick—boot the power and the system."

Gina's voice echoed through the room. "I can't. The house has been disabled from the grid. There is no way to gain access."

Impossible.

Sampson rushed out of the room as a woman's scream pierced the air. "Gina, keep trying!"

Running down the hallway towards the family rooms, he searched for intruders as the power flickered back on. Loyda and Al stood at the entrance to their son's room, their weapons drawn and at the ready. Sampson reached the door to see the nanny knocked out, lying face down. Loyda's face furious amid streaming tears, Al at the busted window staring out into the yard and the most important thing missing…the Smiths' son.

* * * *

Sampson lay with Zasha, kissing her. He opened his mouth to speak, but an incessant beep emerged, with flashing lights from his eyes, over and over until she jerked back in horror. Her arms flailed in the air as she fell off her cot.

She scrambled to a standing position and searched around the room for anything out of place. Blue, red, and white light flashed through the small breaks in the roof slates between the stuffed dry grass. She shivered. No matter what they had done to terraform the damn planet, the air remained as chilly as space.

"Darren," she whispered.

No response came from the mound of blankets on the other cot. She slinked over in a poor attempt at being silent and reached the puffed-up pile of cloth with a huff of frustration. Reaching out, she slapped what would have been his shoulder. Instead, she fell through the configuration of bedding and slammed against the hard cot. Darren was gone.

She scrambled to the holo-screen and opened it up, searching for the last communiqué. Instead, a message remained, typed out for her.

Wipe all trace from the room and meet me at the rendezvous for departure.

The shipping docks? Hell, this wasn't what they'd planned. Though to be honest, she hadn't known the entire rundown. Maybe Kascade had found the earlier scans and the new security system satisfying, and they could head back home.

"Leave no trace, let no one catch you." She mumbled the words under her breath and dread flooded her body. The steady beep from her dream echoed in the real world around her. The lights and the town alarm ensured this would not be a simple exit.

Then a loud speaking voice boomed around her.

"Attention, citizens, an ambassador's child has been kidnapped. Be alert for any suspicious individuals and hold off-worlders for inspection and interrogation."

Damn it to Pluto and back.

Darren did this — he must have — but did Kascade order it? Not possible, not when he wants a successful future for the movement within the APU. Why jeopardize everything by kidnapping someone's kid?

With more questions than answers, she needed to get moving. She plugged in the storage fob stashed in her bracelet, wiped the holo-vid clean of all communication and crashed the hard drive.

Snatching up her bag, she stuffed all her clothes in. She slipped on her grav boots instead of those uncomfortable hemp sandals and grabbed a second bag of stashed weapons. She hoisted everything on her shoulders before she started a wipe down. Leather gloves in place, Zasha ensured no fingerprints were left, employing another program she housed in her scanner. The entire time, she warred with what her heart hoped and what gut instinct told her.

Never believe in coincidences. Her mentor Jennifer had always recited that to her back in the days of the merc guild. *Everything happens for a reason and use those reasons to your advantage and escape.* Chaos, disorder, peace, tranquility—all these states could be used to her advantage.

Though in this case, Zasha needed to blend in, when people were looking for intruders. Once she made it down the ladder, she stripped off the tunic, resituated her bag against her chest, hanging low, and slipped the long red fabric tunic back over her head. The appearance of her carrying a heavy load and being with child might get eyes off her.

She marched out of the back door, slowly moving down the alley and joining the ever-growing crowd.

"What has happened?" Zasha posed this question to a group of women, one of whom eyed her belly and the bag on her back.

"Out late?"

"Returning from a ship just come in on the docks. Visiting my parents." Zasha had learned through random discussions that several of the merchants had daughters and sons off-world. *Knowledge is power.*

The woman hesitated, still taking in her outfit, even the boots. If the damn footwear ruined her lie, then so be it.

Finally, the woman's gaze met hers with an understanding nod. "Well, then you may have got in at a perfect time to avoid this mess. An ambassador's son has been kidnapped. They'll search houses door to door, have no doubt. We might all get interrogated. You best get to your parents' house sooner than later."

Zasha nodded. "My thanks."

She moved steadily but without urgency down the roads, past people searching for suspicious characters and others hoisting themselves from their beds to join the fray. She made her way to the docks, praying Darren hadn't left yet and wondering if he'd gotten caught.

Nothing made a person more fearful of capture than a swarm of law enforcement and crowds of people eager to avoid persecution. Her system profile was less than clean too. She'd killed dozens in her years as a freelance mercenary. Anyone with knowledge of her past might easily leverage her to someone wanting revenge, and her ex-guild would rather kill her than leave her alive in the hands of people who could use what she'd been taught against them.

The docks were ahead of her when the first pup ships flew by overhead, spotlights swooshing back and forth in a crappy search effort. These enforcement types were idiots, believing impounded ships would be safe from thieves. This type of action should have been foreseen.

Her gut churned. *And I helped him do it.*

Somehow her little fake pregnancy act got her safely to the docking area, to the ship they'd agreed on taking when they left, a vessel long impounded for inability to pay a fine or five. It didn't matter really to the APU—the cargo ship was scheduled to be transferred to Titan and dismantled in the junkyard. If the APU couldn't use the tech, they didn't want anyone else to have access to it.

With twin engines and rust in a few key spots, the ship would fly. Zasha's investigation prior to today had verified the most important parts—an operating slip drive and a cloaking system. She keyed into the door and it slid open.

He didn't change the entry code.

She reached into the bag of weapons and grabbed a gun. No way would she head for the main bridge without a little protection. Once there, she spotted Darren, already in a seat and working.

"Tell me you didn't."

"Did you wipe everything as instructed?" Darren never even turned in his chair. This moron underestimated how deadly she could be when the situation called for an executioner.

Zasha frowned, slipping the pack of weapons off her back and to the floor. She grabbed an extra clip for her preferred weapon of choice, a pistol with an automatic setting, custom built—by her.

"Of course I did. Where's the kid?"

Darren still didn't bother to look at her, pressing keys on the panel in front of him, powering up the engines, entering the flight path.

She fired one shot and hit the holo-screen to his right. Sparks emerged, and he leaned backward. He wouldn't need the screen to fly this damn thing.

He won't need anything if he doesn't answer me.

Instead of words, he pushed himself out of his seated position and turned to face her, arms up.

"Where? I won't ask again." The lack of communication only confirmed her gut was right, once more. Being right ranked up there with being stuck in a gravity well—annoying, heartbreaking and lethal.

Darren growled and charged her. Damn if she wasn't regretting this entire venture. She'd wanted to become more involved in Humans First and take on more of a leadership role. Maybe if Kascade became informed of how this idiot had betrayed his efforts, she'd get the chance.

She fired a shot, not wanting to kill. She didn't kill anymore.

Maybe I should.

Because a shoulder hit didn't stop this monster from plowing into her, the gun launching from her hand to the floor and her breath whooshing outward on impact.

Fatch it all.

Chapter Four

"This is why we should have reported her presence here." Lee's frustration was evident by the way she toyed with the knife in her hand.

Sampson wanted to throw back a sarcastic retort, because he couldn't believe the seasoned assassin hadn't bothered to track the mercenary of his dreams in the first place. Lee typically took steps out of precaution before most people considered them. Instead, he shut his mouth and jammed his hand down on the accelerator of the holo-vehicle.

He strongly believed, as Lee did, that whoever had kidnapped Jace would try to get off-world. The APU had locked down all ports, but like Jupiter's main city, this part of Saturn had a port open all hours and constantly in a state of lift-offs and set-downs. This was where the majority of goods came into the western hemisphere of Saturn and where other items, including people, shipped off. They needed to get there fast.

Lee growled again. "She probably had something to do with it. Should have reported her to a pup station as soon as you left the bar. This is going to majorly screw things."

"The obvious isn't wanted right now, Lee. Start scanning those ships as we come over the hill. Let me know which one."

The bracelet on his wrist chimed and he tapped it. "What's up, Gina?"

"The big one, twin engines. The class four cargo shipper. It's your target. They are priming for takeoff, and the ship has a cloak. Once they hit the upper atmosphere, no one will be able to track the vessel."

Lee pointed off to her left. "There it is. Want me to drive, kid?"

"I got it," Sampson snapped. It would be minutes to cross this stretch of terrain, minutes he didn't have, but he focused on what he controlled and the knowledge he possessed. Zasha was here and she never worked alone. "There'll be at least one more."

Lee grinned. "Because mercs work in twos. I had a feeling I wouldn't get out of this trip without stabbing something. Glad to know I'm rewarded for putting up with all of Al's bullshit."

Taking the woman away from bloodthirsty situations didn't take the bloodthirsty out of the woman. Lee always wanted a fight or permission to end life. *Snuff out the bad.* She called it part of her nature. A part Sampson didn't always necessarily agree with, but in this case...

If Zasha had stolen Jace, he'd be sorely tempted. The first, and last, time they'd met hadn't she done the same? Drawn him in close, only to throw a sucker punch when he least expected it? Thankfully he'd recovered, everyone had survived—for the most part— and he wasn't as gullible as he'd once been.

The ship sat dead ahead. The engines were priming, the ignition flames gave a soft whine then a deep rumble shook the ground.

"Gina, any luck hacking in?"

"Nothing. Not my best skill, as you know. I can't break through the APU safeguards either, but they have a containment field in place."

Which didn't mean shit. Containments often failed against payload—put enough extra oomph behind an engine and anyone could bust through a field.

"Then looks like we're the only ones with a chance." He eased up and applied the brake. The vehicle slowed, and they hopped out. They raced towards the loading door, and barely made it inside before the sealing alarms buzzed. Oxygen hissed as pressurization of all areas of the ship started.

Fatch. They were minutes from take-off.

"The bridge." Sampson pointed to the left, and Lee headed out first, twirling her knife. Hell, they didn't have any weapons outside of those knives, Sampson's water torch and a couple of heavy tools.

Sampson snagged a wrench from his tool belt. "Lee."

She nodded at him, and he tossed her the makeshift weapon. She caught it without difficulty. This was how they operated, playing to strengths and leveraging against weaknesses. Sure, Lee didn't necessarily need a weapon, her hands and legs being lethal enough, but an edge never hurt. A knife could be deflected and would work as a distraction for a metal bash to the face.

If they got to the bridge in time, he could possibly prevent this ship from taking off. They had less than two minutes before everything was finalized. He drew and ignited his water torch, ready for an attack. As he made it to his destination, he found Zasha propped on the floor against the side of the doorway, blood dripping down her left cheek.

Sampson switched off the fuel on the torch, tucked it back into his belt and rushed to her side. He gingerly prodded the wound at the top of her head, and she hissed. Protectiveness washed over him in a giant wave. He'd kill the bastard who hurt her. *Absolutely destroy.*

Zasha groaned and batted his hand away, pointing past him. "He's got the kid. Head back that way. Autonav is engaged."

"Sampson!" Lee motioned toward the control panels. "Bigger fish, kid. Leave her and take care of this mess. Which way?"

Zasha pointed down a hallway opposite the way they came. "Ran off there. We got to stop the take-off."

Lee left in the direction Zasha mentioned. "I'll get Jace."

He rushed to the control panels but was too late. Hesitation and eagerness to check on Zasha had zapped Sampson's time. The ship took off, the force against the containment field throwing him off balance and against the floor as the shipper fought gravity.

Then the second engine kicked in and the extra power worked like magic. Free from containment, the ship jetted upward, and Sampson couldn't move. Rarely did *Gina* ever make a landing on a planet for this very reason—take-offs were a bitch, and he wasn't strapped in.

Metal on flesh abraded his back where he lay plastered to the floor. He tried to get a glance at Zasha and failed. Instead, he focused on the next steps. Lee, Zasha's accomplice and Jace were unaccounted for.

He couldn't talk, could barely breathe and had to take shallow breaths. The higher they climbed, the less force weighed against him. Artificial gravity took over as they broke the upper layers of the atmosphere, then they were space bound. A sound of consecutive beeps came from the main computer system, and a glance at the holo-screens showed the cloak going into place. They were truly screwed now.

"Zasha?" Sampson forced himself onto his belly then pushed up on his knees.

She lay flat against the floor, eyes shut.

He crawled toward her. "Hey, wake up."

When she didn't move, he reached out and gently shook her. A tiny notion of fear crept through his skin. Death wasn't an impossibility—head injuries were dangerous. Sure, he wanted revenge for what had happened between them, but not this way.

Her eyes opened and something about those gold irises catching his gaze flooded him with relief. He leaned back, basking momentarily in his thankfulness. She remained alive, even though he'd contemplated having to kill her not more than half a solar hour before. *Such visceral opposing reactions of love and hate, swaying back and forth.* He'd contemplate those things later when they weren't trying to save a kid.

"Did Lee get him?" she asked, as she pushed up on her elbows.

"Who?"

Zasha swiped at her bloody cheek. "Darren. He has the kid. We can't let him keep going."

"The take-off may have incapacitated them."

They helped each other to standing positions. It took a moment to readjust to space, the gravity not as forceful, after being planet-side the better part of a week. Sampson didn't mind this artificial tether. He preferred space.

Zasha moved first, and he followed down the corridor, past the galley, the engine room, other cabins. They got around to the side of the ship where Sampson spied Lee through an open shuttle hatch, passed out on the floor. Sampson pushed Zasha out of the way and jolted forward.

"Sampson, wait!"

He didn't heed her warning. No, he needed to make sure Lee still breathed. No one got the drop on her *ever*. Who the hell was this Darren guy?

"Lee, Lee. Wake up." He shook her shoulders, and she didn't budge.

"Sampson, damn it. This is probably a trap. We can't stay here." Zasha had come up behind him and tapped his boot with hers.

"Help me with Lee." He stood and gripped one of Lee's arms.

Zasha sighed and moved to assist.

That was when an electric current hit him, zapping through Lee's now shoeless body and connecting with him and Zasha. He'd missed her grav boots being gone. Naturally, the boots absorbed electric shocks but this bastard Zasha had aligned with had anticipated the issue.

His hold on Lee failed and he dropped to the floor shaking. The shuttle door sealed shut, oxygen pressurization following within seconds. Then the shuttle ejected. They were sealed away on a four-seater, floating far from the ship and Saturn, headed for wherever space.

Sampson had failed again and this time he only could blame himself as he lay there twitching from the aftershocks of the tasing current.

"Annnnny wayyyy outtt ooof dis?" The electricity caused Zasha to stutter her words.

Sampson willed his arm to move, dragging it up his body and flinging the near-useless appendage over his face to press his nose against the communication bracelet he wore. Amazingly it hadn't shorted out with his extra rubber lining.

Way to think ahead.

"Sampson? What is happening? I don't read you on the planet?" Gina's voice echoed around him like the voice of an angel.

"SOS." The best he could manage before he surrendered to his body's demand for stillness.

"On my way."

* * * *

"She's coming around." This from Gina, whose blue light illuminated a strip of conduit tracing through the middle of every room, hall and spot on the ship. It was a bit creepy, if Zasha dwelled too long about everything Gina saw and heard.

Zasha had always been told that religion existed for the people without skill, talent, or flash, that praying to some god or goddess was the only thing they could rely on when the gold leaves were working against them.

Though she didn't believe in one goddess over them all, she did believe in karma. Whatever a person put out in the universe would visit them again sometime soon…the irony in this little process being how the ship that saved her once had saved her again.

It was something she couldn't pay back, and probably didn't deserve, though the opportunity would give her a chance to maybe make more amends for the betrayals she'd committed years ago. Before she'd learned to be a better person, to be more than a killer.

Zasha pushed up on her elbows and took in the med bay. The last time she'd been here, she'd needed treatment for lack of oxygen. Being inside a ship on fire tended to knock the wind out of a fool. This time she lay recovering from Darren and his *fatching* electric sneak attack.

"Take it slow." Doc's deep voice, the beard — all familiar, though there were more wrinkles around his eyes than last time and more white in his hair.

Is that even possible?

Fatch slow, they needed to move. She needed information and to figure out where things stood before they attacked her. Swinging her legs over the side of the bed, she pushed herself up fully. Her vision immediately blurred as a fresh wave of nausea rose from her stomach.

"Where's Sampson?" she asked, bracing her palms against the bed.

Lee chuckled. "Always worried about the kid and not about yourself. I think we're the ones who need to ask the questions."

Gina spoke at the same time. "He's on the bridge, and I have alerted him about your status."

Relief swirled in her gut. She'd have killed Darren if anything had happened to Sampson. He was good, pure and deserved far more than she'd ever given him. He deserved —

"Where is she?"

Speak of the angel. The handsome man himself had arrived. His ginger hair falling in front of his eyes, he had a shadowy hint of stubble across his jaw, as red as his hair. Sure, he'd looked similar when she'd seen him earlier at the bar, but she'd done a piss-poor job of memorizing the changes. She'd been with him when he hadn't possessed facial hair and now a bit of her below the belt tingled at the idea of his hair-rough skin brushing against her thighs. His tongue... *Fatch.*

"I'm here." She cleared her throat. Did her voice sound deep and sultry?

Damn it. Be serious. They might kill you.

Even when they were enemies, when he hated her, her body had still wanted him.

"We should turn her over to the pups. Let Al know she's got the details on his son and leave straight away." This from Lee, who by all rights, had never trusted or liked her.

Killers always sense other killers.

"How did Darren get the drop on you, Lee?" Zasha threw out the insulting question with mustered sarcasm.

Provoking criminals and villains is a last resort. Another Jennifer gem, one her old mentor had never followed.

The assassin frowned and marched over to her. "With some sneak-attack bullshit. The kid was in the shuttle when I happened by. Maybe the fool considered abandoning ship, but he doesn't care about the kid. Launched a canister of sleeping gas at me. Not very sporting, but your buddy is an idiot."

"Why?"

Lee pulled out a knife and stuck it into the table right next to Zasha's hand, less than a half-inch away. "He left me alive."

Shit, the kid might be already dead too. Sleeping gas was dangerous to fully grown humans. A little went a long way.

Sampson pulled the knife out of the table, stood in front of her and angled the sharp tip towards Zasha's throat. Suddenly, the Sampson she'd known appeared a distant memory to this violent human unafraid to threaten her life. His grip on the knife remained firm, probably thanks to Lee's tutelage, though Zasha could disarm him if he really wanted to hurt her.

"Who's Darren? Why did you steal the Smiths' kid? Give me one reason we don't turn you over to the pups right now." Sampson moved the knife closer, less than a quarter-inch from her neck and those damn things were sharp.

Zasha took a deep breath and opted for the truth. "Darren is a member of Humans First. He and I were sent to Saturn to exchange some messages with allies toward the cause and pick up supplies. Yesterday, we received direction to scope out the Smiths' home to ensure security and safety for our leader, Kascade, who planned to meet with Al Smith. I have no clue why Darren took the kid instead, but you can't throw me to the pups because you need me. I know where Darren went."

Sure, some of the words were liberties. She didn't have all the details, but Kascade always preached about harmony, finding common roads and showing people the way to peace even when opposed. There would be no reason for Kascade to resort to kidnapping. So, until she found evidence stating otherwise, she'd blame the kid's disappearance on Darren.

"Where did he go?" Sampson's green eyes were homed in on her, the knife remained at her neck.

Zasha's sense of conscience warred within her. One of the reasons Humans First had survived so long, even with the APU hailing them as a terrorist organization, was because no one possessed the location or access to their facility.

Darren really was an idiot, because he should have killed her too. No way would she allow him to threaten everything Humans First worked for or stood by and let him sacrifice a kid for the cause. Killing children only started revenge vendettas, and never ended with benefits.

She struggled with the possibility that Kascade had given the order and if the Smiths' kid turned out to be the goal the entire time, then everything she'd worked for would be a lie.

The peaceful man who'd spoken eloquently on fighting for the rights of the lower planets, of working together to find solutions to end the reliance on human bones for ship fuel… Even *Gina* used the same type of propulsion and Zasha found the reality disheartening, that the death of others powered travel across space.

The knife's tip touched her throat, metal against breakable skin, forcing Zasha back to the present. If she had tears to shed, she would at her ex-lover's menacing scowl.

Sampson growled. "Where?"

She swallowed, enjoying the tiny bit of pain, awaiting the separation of her flesh, the free flow of blood and welcoming the death to follow. Death was too good a fate for a killer like her, but she'd no longer live with her sorrows.

Don't I deserve worse for what I did to them eight years ago?

"To Earth's moon."

Chapter Five

They laid a course for the moon and Sampson ditched Zasha in the med-bay, refusing to look at the small drop of blood she had on her neck. He swallowed down his revulsion, as he did with every small piece of violence he executed, and warred with himself for daring to hurt her, wanting to hurt her. Love and wrath truly went hand in hand between them.

Briefly, he'd sought more than reasons for their present problems, but he wanted revenge for all the nights he'd cried, for the hours spent wishing she'd done things differently. He also wished she hadn't tried to kill him mere solar hours after telling him she loved him.

At the same time, he wanted to hold her, press kisses to her cheeks and breathe in her scent of metal and ozone. Yes, damn weird to be attracted to such a thing, but she had a natural space smell to her hair and skin, as though she'd been born from the universe and existed only to slowly poison him to all other things.

Fatch it all to hell and back.

He left her to Lee and Doc, with the instructions she be monitored and given a chance to clean up. Though those two wouldn't do her any favors. Animosity still existed in every member of the crew toward her.

Hopefully, she'd get the hell out of those fake clothes. The tunic didn't fit her. He needed her strapped in her vest, belt and matching pants. He remembered the off-shoulder sweater she used to wear belted around her waist. Shit, there were memories upon memories. Two weeks of every waking, and some sleeping moments, wrapped up in someone who had imprinted on him for the rest of his life.

Gina's light blinked and her voice intoned, "I have made the connection. Incoming holo-vid with Loyda and Al Smith."

The screen in front of Sampson filled with the concerned faces of two people who'd trusted him.

"Where is Jace?" Al demanded, those eyebrows of his hunched and his gaze full of menace.

Loyda's eyes were red and puffy, though she'd dabbed away any tears.

Sampson had done his fair share of tear shedding in the past, and his news might bring more. "We believe he's in a cloaked shipper en route to the moon. Gina has set a course and we hope to intercept—"

"I'm sending an APU cruiser straightaway." Al wanted immediate action.

Sampson sighed. "Listen, I don't think a cruiser is a good idea. We're not sure what these people are capable of—if this is a ransom or a planned murder."

Loyda stifled a cry, and Al roared as he pounded his fists against the table in front of him. "You're upsetting my wife."

Sampson was thankful they were far from Saturn at the moment. "All I'm asking for is time. Gina has a course plotted, and we'll be there within three solar days with no stops. We're stocked, fueled and can get there with speed. You trusted me with the job to protect your family, so let me finish it."

Silence reigned as both Al and Loyda turned from the screen. The communication between them remained nonverbal, all gazes, gentle hand squeezes and Al's soft kiss pressed to Loyda's forehead.

How Sampson desired the ability to love someone, be so close to them words weren't needed to convey what needed to be said. The one person he'd believed might be that other half was half a ship away and he still wanted to tear at her as much as hug her. *Snap the hell out of it*, he ordered himself.

"All right." Loyda faced the screen first. "We'll give you three solar days. If your communication on the third day does not yield an appearance of my son, you won't get paid for your work on the system, and a cruiser will be dispatched along with my husband."

Sampson nodded in agreement. "Fine. I accept the terms."

Al cleared his throat. "If I have to come out there, I can't promise I won't make an enemy of my sister again, but know this, nothing happens to my son."

The communication cut off before Sampson could respond. "Did you end that, Gina?"

"No." Her blue light blinked around him. "The Smiths did. Three days is cutting the deadline short. I'll need you to monitor things, especially with the pressure levels in the drive as we travel."

"We've got this. Now, I need food." Sampson pushed out of his chair on the bridge and nodded to Dottie. "Need anything?"

Dottie, the ship's official pilot—though Gina did most of the work—shook her head, her eyes never leaving the screen in front of her. "No, except…maybe someone to do relief duty in an hour or so. With that merc walking the ship, we can't risk leaving the bridge exposed. I know Gina has plenty of attention on the matter, but I want to take extra precautions."

"Agreed. We can't take any risks this round." No matter what happened next, Zasha's presence on this ship put everyone on high alert. "All right, I'll be back." He left for the galley, easily able to find his path because Gina trailed him, her blue light coming awake in a low hum section by section as he went. "What's wrong?"

"I am easy to detect?"

"Always." He was in tune with every sound, chirp and color she made.

"Zasha's presence has elevated the blood pressure of everyone on the ship. Lee is casually clenching her jaw, Doc is shifting with tension in his shoulders and Dottie more focused. How does a person influence people this way?"

She left out the part about his violent actions, but he appreciated her not calling him out.

"You have a longer, clearer memory than I do, Gina. She betrayed us, attacked us on Io, killed a scientist, almost killed the crew and tried to steal the capsule that created Sweet's planet."

The galley lay ahead, and once inside, Sampson immediately got into the cooler stores, pulling out freeze-dried vegetables, fruits and meats they'd packed from Eden, the small APU-free planet he'd just mentioned. *Where Emilio and Toni are probably headed at this moment.*

The blue light turned green, a symbol of Gina's confusion. "I recall these events. Though, I also have in my databanks her message. She apologized for her behavior."

"Sometimes apologies aren't enough." This came from Lee who walked in, rushed over to Sampson and stole a handful of berries from his plate.

"Yes, and humans lie, from what I have previously recorded. I will keep a close watch."

"Eyes in the back of your head." Lee popped a berry into her mouth. "We all need to have them."

Sampson didn't miss Lee's pointed stare and word emphasis. "I'm well aware."

"Are you?" Lee stepped in close. "She pulls a knife on you, primes a weapon, runs sabotage...it's gonna take more than holding a knife to her throat and a drop of blood. You need to be willing to go all the way."

He took a deep breath, despising the anxious energy coursing his veins, the quickening of his pulse at the images Lee conjured in his brain, dark, twisted shit of Zasha at his feet, arms outstretched, blood pouring from her throat. The gurgling of unintelligible words. *Fatch.*

"If she plans to ambush us, my calculations predict more success once we pass Jupiter, but before we get into the asteroid belt." Gina's pure logic cut through the pounding of blood in his ears.

He pushed past Lee and shoved himself into a seat at the center table.

"Thanks for the reminder, Gina. Though I would do something in the asteroid belt. Send out a second ship.

Just my thought process." Lee chuckled, and Sampson couldn't meet her enthusiasm for plotting subterfuge or murder.

Hell, he wanted this to be easy. Why did everything get so damn complicated?

"I would agree on the asteroid belt. Less likely to send out an SOS or have more ships passing by who would bother to stop." Zasha's voice washed over him, chill bumps breaking out over his arms, and Sampson struggled to focus on finishing his plate instead of her.

How had he not noticed she acted a lot more like Lee than the sweet, fellow engineer he'd taken her for in the beginning? Talk of betrayal and double-cross so easily rolled off her tongue. *Enraging.*

Except her metal tang filled his nostrils. The scent acted like a siren's call, which made his hands either want to grip flesh or tools. He dropped his plate onto the galley table. A couple of grapes rolled off, and Lee snatched them up. Sampson filled his mouth with food and kept silent for a minute, long enough for Zasha to move farther into the room. His attempt to clear his thoughts failed horribly. Finally, he managed to grab on to one thing.

"Could we focus on the real goal? Not double-crosses and bullshit—it's getting to the moon, recovering the kid." Sampson bit into a grape, letting the juice coat his tongue. Normally he'd relish the sweet and tart flavor. Only as another scent filled his nostrils did he dare to glance at Zasha. She stood across from him, outfitted in her regular attire. His dick hardened immediately in his pants. The grape's taste died then and there. He should hate her.

I do hate her. Then, why do I want her so bad?

* * * *

Zasha took a seat at the galley table, grabbing for an empty mug in the center and the pot. She remembered the standard hot water kept for all the crew members and the instant granule imitation-coffee-crap in the red jar beside the kettle. *The closest to the real stuff a person got, next to smuggling in the shit from Earth.* She poured the water, dumped in the granules and kept her focus on the brown kernels transforming into caffeine-laden liquid fuel. Her mentor had said time and again that coffee was worse than drugs but provided more awareness than any drug could give.

Sampson continued to work on his plate, Lee stood leaning against a counter, and no one spoke. The debate warred within her to spout more apologies, though so far words of remorse appeared ineffective. She could recite the speech she'd played out over and over in her head.

How she'd learned from her mistakes. How she stopped seeking revenge through punishing others and found comfort in helping those with less, though Darren's bullshit failed to help anyone see she'd grown and failed to help her association with Humans First appear more than standard merc work. The silence continued and Zasha bounced between short glances at Sampson and staring into her coffee mug.

He appeared frustrated. Hell, everyone acted the same way with varying physical tics.

"Sampson, I'll need that tune-up now. We are going to pick up speed shortly thanks to a curve in the current." Gina's light blinked in unison with her words, ending the official silence.

Zasha slammed back the weak-ass cup of coffee she'd made. The liquid wasn't hot, merely warm. The work presented another opportunity to talk with Sampson, a chance to get through to him. She stood. "I can help."

"We won't all fit down there," Lee growled.

Zasha almost rolled her eyes. The engine room wasn't super big, but if anything went wrong, she wouldn't make it out alive. Zasha feared the ship over Lee, who could be influenced by other opinions, including her own.

"I won't try anything. I want to help. Whether you believe me or not, I don't agree with Darren taking the kid and I didn't know anything about a kidnapping." Zasha directed her words to Sampson, who'd been rather quiet after mentioning double-crosses.

She didn't expect any more surprises but wouldn't have put it past Darren to have something rigged and waiting. Humans First had become notorious over the years for keeping their methods and actions to themselves, beyond their location, and they had allies everywhere. One wouldn't think so, but the majority of humanity didn't like sacrificing their loved ones after death to become fuel for ships they'd never ride in.

Sampson glanced up at her, and their eyes met. The flecks of gold in his stood out more when he came. *Oh.* The memory appeared in her mind unbidden, and her cheeks grew hot.

Sampson raised one eyebrow, but she didn't miss the momentary question in his gaze. "Fine, you can come with. But only to assist. Try anything and —"

"Gina will fry me. I know."

Lee chuckled. "He was going to say I would kill you."

"I can fry people? Sampson, what would this entail?"

Gina's question brought a smile to Zasha's face. "She doesn't know the kind of power she possesses?" Zasha placed her empty cup on the table.

Sampson shook his head. "She does but chooses not to use the capability. Either way, if Gina doesn't take care of you, Lee will. Lee, can you relieve Dottie? Since I'm doing this, someone will need to help on the bridge."

The assassin gave a low growl of acknowledgment and bumped into Zasha as she walked past. Zasha budged a little, allowing the movement to give Lee a false sense of security. Once the assassin cleared out, Zasha refocused.

"So, you are in charge?" she couldn't help asking. He'd been the one giving commands and for some reason, his 'take-charge' voice awakened her emotions all over again. Sampson had been the kid, the help. Now he appeared so much more.

"This mission is mine. So, yes everyone is following my lead." Sampson stood up, tall and straight, and walked his plate over to the sink.

"Impressive." She gave a grin, enjoying how he puffed up in response.

He scrubbed the plate with a soap brush and ran it through the waterspout before putting the ceramic dish into a drainer. "I work as hard as everyone else, and I'm capable of doing what needs to be done. Being in charge is a natural progression."

Zasha moved in closer to him, under the guise of putting her mug in the sink. "Maybe, but I remember how you liked taking orders once."

His eyes flashed with anger. "I give them now and wash your damn cup. We don't clean up other people's messes on this ship."

He stomped away from her, and she couldn't deny the heat flooding her core at how he talked. Her body tingled with his words. She liked new and improved Sampson, even if his rough, brisk manner meant he'd never let her get close. Not after what had happened.

Doesn't mean I won't try.

She couldn't waste an opportunity to change his mind, to see about earning the redemption she craved above all else. She took over at the sink and scrubbed the mug clean. Once finished, she put it in the drain pan and turned around to find him watching her, waiting at the door.

He'd done the same a long time ago too, though with less scowl and more grin. As soon as dishes were finished from a meal they would run off and explore the ship. Tinkering here, making out there... Shit. "I'm ready if you are."

Sampson turned on his heel without a word, a silent command to follow and, like a good, desperate sycophant, she did.

After about ten steps, he spoke. "What were you thinking about back there?"

"Memories. Being back on this ship keeps sparking things I'd forgotten about. You and me—"

"Yeah, I get what you mean." He came to a halt, and her front brushed up against his back. He hissed at the contact, and she near moaned. *Fatch.* This couldn't be good.

"Forgot my tools. Come on," Sampson turned on his heel, and Zasha despaired at how he dismissed whatever sparked between them. No matter how negative his emotions were toward her, the attraction remained. She could build off the hint of this desire.

Sampson broke out into a jog, a futile escape tactic, and she kept pace with nimble, tiptoe strides. They came to a stop at one of the cabin doors. It slid open and revealed a new world to her.

Sampson had always slept in a bunk near Gina's engine, a small room across from the med bay. It had once been a closet but transformed so he could be close if there were problems with the engine or the computer processors.

Now, he'd officially grown up. Crossing the threshold, Sampson held up a hand for her to remain there.

"I can't come in?"

He glanced back at her, the pain in his eyes clear. "No, not in this space."

She hated how her gut clenched at his words. This place remained untainted by her presence. *Why bother ruining things by allowing me inside?* It hurt a bit, but she deserved such things.

Sampson grabbed his toolset from a chair positioned outside the bathroom and strapped it to his waist. He grabbed a small box as well, hefting the kit as if it were lighter than air and handed it to her as he stepped outside the door.

"I'm not here to hurt you, Sampson." *At least not intentionally.* She couldn't stop the words from flowing forth. She wanted to clarify things, make him realize that this time she needed him for more than what he could do with his hands…though, his hands would be an extra benefit.

"Were you planning to kidnap the baby for a ransom? Or sell the kid to the highest bidder?"

She frowned and her shoulders dropped. Sampson pushed past her, heading for the rear of the ship where the engine and core processors existed in harmony.

Zasha followed him, trying to stay silent, but unable to in the face of lies lobbed at her. "This did not happen with my knowledge. I never planned to take the kid. I'm not a trafficker. Never have been and trading flesh is more disgusting than killing."

"Tell your lies to the indentured workers for the BCS and the APU. Anything reviled only means it costs more. You say you didn't plan this, but I don't know what you're into any longer. You were so good at lying before. I can't imagine the devious part of you has changed."

"You mean you *won't* imagine it," she mumbled following behind him. She alternated the toolbox between her hands and debated hurling the hunk of metal at the back of his stubborn head.

Maybe a good concussion will wake him up.

"I'm not here to get the kid for my purposes. Hell, I wouldn't be here at all if Darren had left the kid alone. Whatever Darren has planned, this child doesn't deserve that. The Smiths don't. No one does. Besides, taking the kid defeats the purposes of my organization. How does stealing a child help the APU see how using dead people for space travel is wrong? I can't believe our leader would sign off on this.

"With all our technology and power, we still haven't come up with something more invested, longer-lasting. We're encouraging our own extinction. Humans First wants to educate those blind and ignorant. Think positive, think light, believe trust."

She sighed, breathing heavily as they came to a stop right outside the engine room. The door slid open, the steady hum of the slip drive much louder now.

Sampson turned to face her, taking the toolbox from her hands. The brief connection made her fingers itch to grab him back. To hold him close to her.

"What kind of crappy motto is that?"

She shrugged. "The kind to make a person keep getting up the next day and hoping for a better tomorrow."

Sampson chuckled. "Really? Sounds like some brainwashing stuff."

"What do I have to do to prove myself to you?" The question came with a touch of desperation. She should have held back a little, but his constant animosity grated her last nerve.

"I don't know, Zasha. You kind of fatched all my goodwill when you tried to blow us up on Io."

"If I wanted you dead, you wouldn't be breathing now." She clenched her fists, as Sampson took in a sharp breath.

"That right there...you don't see anything wrong with your actions. Everything is justified." His eyes took on a gleam, like a bright light illuminating a dark space. "Ya know what I think?"

She crossed her arms and huffed. "No clue, but I bet you'll tell me."

"You and Darren got in an argument on the ship, probably who would get credit or, knowing you, pissed off that Darren caused an area-wide alert. He got the drop on you, and now Gina is your only way back to the fold."

Her gaze softened and her arms dropped to her sides as she met his arrogant stare. He'd grown old and jaded, where once he'd been innocent, bright-eyed, kind and ready to offer help to whomever. She'd contributed to this, and her stomach churned with nausea. *Though if Sampson can create these types of stories in his head, what about Kascade?* She needed to stop the same thing from happening there, from the truth being twisted merely by her past actions.

"No, I'm on this ship because it's the only way I can stop Kascade, our leader, and the Humans First movement from being dragged into some mess by an idiot."

"Speaking lies doesn't make them true, but you go ahead and say what you want, hoping it will save your skin." Sampson set the toolbox on the floor at her feet, kneeling before it. She followed, wanting to be as close to him as he would allow.

She reached for the handle of the lid, pulling it back for him right after he unlatched the lock. "Then why don't you kill me already?"

"I don't have a reason to...yet." His eyes were on the tools, searching for something.

She grabbed the screwdriver and held it up to him. "Oh, I'd say you have plenty of reasons. Me almost killing you in that scientist's workshop being the top one. So, do it. Let your hatred out physically, if you can't let it go with words."

His head rose, the very emotion she claimed reflected back at her. "Why do you keep pushing this? I'm already reaching my limit."

"Because I don't want to lose someone else to the pitch, but I'm not going to keep fighting a pointless cause."

The flames of vengeance died out, his scowl lessened and he asked, "What's the pitch?"

She let the screwdriver fall back into the box. "The pitch is the dark parts of us that eat up what little humanity we have left, slowly taking away the light inside us, the thing driving us to help others, to do better. I already took so much, from so many. I took the same light from you."

He broke eye contact and started to rummage in the array of doohickeys and thingamabobs. She recognized half of the stuff there but would be embarrassed to admit her tool and tech knowledge barely compared to Sampson's.

She clenched her fingers against her knees, anxious to hold something, in fear of his response.

The clanking and rustling in the toolbox stopped. Sampson looked up at her and for a brief moment, she saw it, the old him. The kindness emerged, and he reached up and stroked her cheek. He smelled of machine oil, rust and a tang like iron-filled blood. She loved his scent. She'd loved him. *Never stopped.*

"How can I trust you? Trust myself?"

Without a second thought, she leaned closer. "This between us isn't a lie."

As their lips touched, a surge of energy arced between them like an electrical storm shooting across the skies of Mars. She'd seen the storms once, on Mars, on Jupiter, Io…anywhere with an atmosphere where ions collided. They were the ions now, sparking off each other, first with their lips then their tongues.

Then he bit her lip, the sting and true taste of blood hitting her tongue. She pulled back and scrambled to stand.

Sampson didn't move, still down on his knees. He gave her a long gaze, hard once more, before he put his focus back on the toolbox. "I think you're wrong. I think we're all in the pitch and every time we try to crawl out something...*someone* is sent to remind us we don't deserve anything more."

She shook her head. He couldn't see, but she did nonetheless. "No, I can't agree with such hopelessness. Sampson, I get forgiveness is far from being on the table. I want to earn it somehow, but I do need you to trust me, or this won't work."

Sampson laughed and tossed the tool in his hand in the air. He rose as the double-headed welding wrench screeched against the cold air, the metal already heating with the head exposed from its cooling cover. Snatching the wrench up dulled the sound.

"You tell the best jokes."

Zasha frowned. "It's the truth, not a joke."

Sampson leaned in close to her again and an iron tang filled her nostrils, matching what she still tasted on her lips. Heat bloomed between them, but she couldn't tell whether it was from the wrench or the heavy pull they held over each other.

"Then you know it's impossible." He turned away and stalked into the engine room, and Zasha took a deep breath.

"Nothing is impossible." She proclaimed to the space in front of her.

She didn't miss Gina's blue light blink.

Chapter Six

Alarms rang out, more beeping sounds, flashing lights. Gina's voice echoing, "Alert, alert. All hands."

Zasha woke startled, vestiges of a burning ship in her mind's eye.

Eight years prior, she'd woken to fire flaming around her, her pilot and merc partner dead, everything red hot, eating all the oxygen, and no chance to flee with the escape pods already launched. A death-ensured disaster she'd survived because Sampson had heard her distress call and saved her.

As if called by her memories, when she opened her eyes, Sampson hovered over her, shaking her gently by her shoulders.

"Zasha, come on. An APUP ship stopped us — we're going to be boarded. We reached the asteroid belt checkpoint, but they didn't let us pass."

Her eyes shot open, and she sat up fully, Sampson's hold on her arms loosening as she rose. "An ambush."

"Maybe. I'm not sure. Of course, Lee thinks so, and we're prepared for this."

Zasha rubbed at her eyes, wiping away the images of her fire nightmares. "You're working for the Smiths, so you should have clearance. Anything else is suspect."

Sampson sighed. "You're right. As usual."

"I've got the mind for this kind of crap. Where is everyone?"

Sampson stood up from the bed, taking a few steps away toward the door. "Everyone is gathered on the bridge, and we need to join them."

She'd been given a cabin of her own. Close to Sampson's, but still guarded and locked by Gina. She couldn't get anywhere without the AI knowing anything and she hadn't wanted to. No, after messing with the engine, and helping Sampson ensure the slip drive held up, she'd been in desperate need of a shower.

She'd taken in the ionic waves and fallen right to sleep afterward. Of course, she'd changed into only a shirt and underwear, and now Sampson got to see everything too.

"I'll be there if you can give me a few minutes."

His gaze glued itself to her bare legs and trailed up her figure. "Yes…the bridge. I'll be outside the door."

He marched out of her quarters as if he fought against the pull of a gravity well.

Zasha couldn't help but smile, even though there were bigger monsters to fry at the moment and she needed her full wardrobe. She'd been too tired to mess with the ion wash for those, so her clothes were less than pristine, but she managed to get herself locked and loaded. *Can't really be loaded with no weapons. Something I need to remedy.*

Outside her door, Sampson paced. "Ready?"

She nodded, and they took off.

Sampson beat her with the width of his stride, easily two to three steps ahead at all times. "Gina, update?"

"They have sent over the correct codes. I double-checked them. Everything appears legitimate. I've extended the boarding tunnel."

"Have everyone except Dottie meet me at the entrance."

Zasha huffed as she tried to extend her gait to keep up. "So much for meeting on the bridge."

The message didn't take long to spread, and soon Doc and Lee flanked them right beside the entrance hatch. Lee tapped Zasha on the shoulder and extended the butt of an old revolver to her.

"You might want this."

"Appreciate it—you gave me the oldest weapon known to humanity except for the knife and club."

"Better than nothing," Lee replied with a grin.

Zasha flipped open the cylinder and sighed. "And one bullet."

Gina's light went yellow. "Seal confirmed. Pressurization complete."

The hatch opened with a familiar *snick* and slide then the pups marched in. Six strong, weaponized with laser guns and primed. They aimed and fired. No words, no offers to surrender, just open season on the innocent. Sampson was one of the first to drop. Zasha saw red and leveled the barrel at the large bastard, but the gun jammed.

Fatch you, Lee.

The assassin and Doc were helpless against these weapons. Sure, Lee injured one in the leg before going down, but otherwise they were all fixed stars. She couldn't do much but chuck the shitty gun at the nearest suited-up spacehole.

She aimed for the helmet and the jerk dodged, then stopped charging. "Hold fire."

He grabbed Zasha's arm, his brute strength forcing her to stay still, and pulled up the sleeve of her shirt to expose her Humans First tattoo.

Then he released her before shedding his helmet. Fists at the ready she was seconds from launching at him.

The spacehole spoke as he lifted his arm and the familiar sight of the Humans First symbol appeared. "We're here to help. He said you would be coming."

Her hands were still tightened, locked and ready to fire, but she relaxed her stance. Her body reflected her mind, warring between wanting to react to this bastard shooting Sampson and to embrace the cessation.

She glanced at Sampson's prone body, with its ginger locks lifeless against his forehead. Then his body twitched, so did Doc's and Lee's.

"Stun shots?"

"Yeah, though a little higher than the basic level. We needed some extra oomph. Was told this group might cause trouble."

Zasha let those words wash over her and tried to quell the anger flooding her system. She envisioned the rage flowing to her clenched fists and releasing from her body as she opened her palms.

Sampson groaned in pain on the floor, and none of it mattered. She'd find out the plan these pups had then get rid of them.

Humans First or not, this time I choose Gina and the crew.

Though, she couldn't take down this group alone. "Yeah, who told you?"

"Darren. He reached out to us and wanted us to take action. Stop the ship at a checkpoint and make sure they don't get by were the instructions. We had to give Darren a head-start back to base and can't let others find us."

Zasha considered the big pup. "What's your name?"

"Eek, short for Ezekiel. Never liked the name. Pups gave me this shorter one."

Well, he won't need a name for long.

"Eek, did Darren give you the download on what's happening?"

"Finishing a mission up on Saturn and said you were hitching a ride in disguise with these guys. We were to rescue you and send the rest to BCS salvage."

Over my dead body.

Eek glanced at her fallen companions. "Is there anyone else on the ship?"

"Yeah, a pilot. Head to the bridge. I need to gather my things and I'll meet you back here."

Eek nodded agreement, choosing to go voice silent, and urged his pals forward with hand signals. Zasha wanted to shoot then, each one right in the back. *Fatch staring them straight in the face and lying.* She wanted to scream her fury at Darren, these pups and the whole stupid mission...though this experience had taught her new things. Humans First had allies in the pups and at the highest levels of society. *What next? An army of ships I don't know about.*

We need to get out of this mess.

"Gina, can you zap them?"

The ship's blue light blinked. "Not without hitting you as well."

"Then convince them not to leave yet. Hold off the BCS until I can get everyone awake."

"I'm not supposed to speak."

Zasha recalled why. Sampson had told her the story of Gina's fall, where several moonies from one of the moon bases planted malware into her AI and almost destroyed her. She'd been taught to mimic the silence of other ships around people she couldn't trust. The fact she spoke to Zasha at all served as a reminder of how the AI had some trust in her, which blossomed in Zasha's chest, along with a smidge of hope.

She leaned down and caressed Sampson's cheek. "He's gonna think I did this."

The blue tint from Gina's light shone brightly. "Then I'll correct him, but we must move quick. They have subdued Dottie, and we need a plan."

* * * *

His mouth was dry like he'd been left out on Mars with no mask — the red dirt tended to coat every surface it contacted. Opening his eyes was a struggle, like peeling sticky tape from a roll. Sampson tried to lean backward and move his arms, with no luck. *Tied tight.* He sat in one of the egg-shaped chairs in *Gina's* galley. The others were all present, except for Zasha.

"Do I get to say I called it?" Lee's voice rose from his left, and he forced his head to turn in her direction.

"No."

"Come on," she groaned. "I said they would ambush us after Jupiter."

No, Zasha had called it on cue. Had she been trying to warn him, and he had been too stupid to get it? Here they sat tied up. How many times would he potentially be at the mercy of people trying to kill him?

"Dottie, are you okay?" Doc's concerned voice broke Sampson from his pity party and he glanced from the older man to the woman who'd stolen Doc's heart.

She lifted her head and gave a small smile. "I'm fine. We've had worse."

"Has anyone seen Zasha?" The last thing Sampson recalled was hitting the floor before he'd passed out. *Electric bolts do that to a person.*

Dottie, Doc and Lee all shook their heads.

"Do you think they killed her?" Because the idea she'd betrayed them warred within him. Though when they'd conversed the day before in the hallway, she'd been so earnest...damn determined to make him see this trustworthy side of her. He'd slept fitfully, his tossing and turning remnants of his constant confused emotions.

"We wouldn't be so lucky," Lee sassed back.

This conversation would go nowhere, not with the continued animosity. Sampson settled with attempting to communicate with Gina to get them out of this mess. For the sake of saving herself, she'd remain verbally silent. The ship could do a lot, but people who discovered her capabilities either wanted to possess or destroy her. She'd been threatened too many times for being more than a simple ship.

Sampson worked his legs up into the chair, taking deep breaths the entire way. With a little patience and time, he got his arms in front of him.

"Agile as always." Lee had already done the same, and she'd begun to awkwardly walk the chair back toward the galley counter, not far from the knives.

Sampson simply wanted to get a response from Gina. To find out where Zasha was and see if there was an option to incapacitate the pups. He made tap after tap in Morse code on the table in front of him—an old communication system used on Earth back before anyone had dreamed of space travel. He had studied it and taught Gina.

The blinking lights of her communication system sent a response more confusing than being blasted by a stun ray less than a day after being tased.

We are okay, caught in the pup checkpoint still, but working fast.

Who is working fast? He messaged back.

Zasha and me. Get ready—when we move it will be quick. Tell Lee to stop trying to escape.

"Lee, Gina says to hold."

She growled, her hands still sawing back and forth through the bonds around her legs. "Hold? Let these bastards continue doing whatever, I don't think so."

"We need to trust her. I trust her."

"Trust?" Lee's voice level started to rise. "Trust? You would let a woman who stomped on your heart kiss you in a corridor and get close all over again. I don't know if your judgment is the best right now."

Sampson slapped his palms against the table. "How do you know about that and why is it your business?"

"It's my business to make sure you don't make mistakes that cost the rest of us our lives."

Anger flooded through him. She still treated him like a child. Hell, they all did. Doc and Dottie didn't voice any disagreement.

"Emilio and Toni put me in charge—"

"Oy! What's happening in here?" A pup guard entered the room.

Fatch.

Lee laughed, loud and annoying. "What's going on is the kid next to you has got his pants in a twist because we won't follow him blindly like we do our regular co-captains. He's not the wisest person in the land, even if he can re-assemble a ship busted in under a solar day."

The pup chuckled, then sobered at the mention of Sampson's talents. "No one can fix a ship that fast."

Lee stuck her tongue out and winked at him. "He really can."

Fatch you, Sampson mouthed back at her.

The pup leaned in close to him. "Then why aren't you working for the APU on one of those cruisers?"

"Because"—Sampson sat up a little straighter, his arms tucked in his lap, but the pup didn't seem to be paying too close attention. Idiots—"I can't stand assholes."

The fool let out a belly-aching laugh, exposing his stomach. Sampson moved in. He shoved his head into the pup's pudgy midsection, then upward, connecting with the pup's chin, followed by another heavy-hitting punch to the jaw. The idiot crumpled and fell to the floor.

Lee already free, bonds snapped, moved to the body. She broke the fool's neck with a simple twist, no hesitation.

Sampson should have shuddered, twinged in guilt, but nothing came. He had no sympathy for these men, though this dead pup wasn't the one who'd zapped him.

Zasha's face popped in the doorframe. "Damn it, Lee. Why did you kill him?"

Lee, the pup's gun now in hand, trained the barrel on Zasha as she tossed a knife to Sampson. "Because I want to make an example of people who want to hurt me and mine."

"Fatch it all, but I had a plan to get us out of here without bloodshed. I needed him."

Gina's blue light illuminated once more. "She did have a good one, and I'm afraid we may have put a kook in it."

"A kook? You mean *kink*. What is the plan?" Sampson had already freed himself and moved to Dottie first, followed by Doc, who immediately swept to his beloved's side to inspect her himself.

"They were drinking. I drugged them with some of Doc's sleeping pills. Your noise brought this one here before he drank to the toast of capturing this vessel and your crew."

Dread filled Sampson at the pit of his stomach. "Why would they be happy to capture us?"

Zasha moved into the room and over to the dead guard. "I may have encouraged them to research the ship and crew instead of rushing to turn you over to BCS salvage."

Holy hell. They'd flown under the radar for more than a year but had still hit the tops of wanted lists. Gina could mask their appearance most times but moving at fast speeds sometimes took away the capability. *Shit.*

"Did they report us?"

"Yes and no. The report's written, not sent. They passed out before then. I was coming to grab this guy and now he's dead." Zasha reached down and put one of the guy's dead arms around her shoulders. "Help me get him to the boarding tunnel. We can place them all on the umbilical and call it a day. Though with one of them dead, when the others wake, I can't promise your crew won't be blamed."

Lee shrugged, still pointing her gun at Zasha. "Not like we aren't wanted now. Nothing changes."

"Yes, but I never intended to bring more attention to us." Sampson moved to help Zasha with the guard.

The pair of them began the struggling walk and drag out of the galley and back to the entrance of the hatch where the pups had come in. He didn't say anything as they moved, but he could see her glances. She wanted to speak, and he refused to encourage her.

She'd chosen to help them, but why? Why hadn't she been shot like them? There were questions and no time for answers. They needed a way out of this mess.

They had almost made it halfway when Lee sighed and picked up the legs of the dead guy.

"You two take too long. We got to move him and those others. Let's haul. Never know when their next check-in is supposed to happen, and we need to be long gone."

Her words helped them move their asses, transporting bodies to the umbilical then disconnecting the damn thing from the ship. Once the hatch closed, Sampson glanced at Lee with a silent question. She gave him a single nod.

He marched past Zasha back toward the bridge. Doc and Dottie were already there. "Do we?"

Doc nodded. "Yes, for punishment. Who knows how many others?"

Sampson agreed, but wanted the others to align as well. "Gina, blow the checkpoint."

"Yes, sir."

Zasha came running up behind him, her boots echoing across the ship walls. She grabbed his shoulder. "What are you doing? Gina and I were going to electrocute the umbilical—they'd wake with fuzzy memories and no clue if what happened was true."

Sampson shrugged her off. "We're getting rid of these pups, this checkpoint. No mercy."

Gina's cannon, a new addition within the last year, started to prime. The weapon functioned as an EMP or incendiary device with a laser capable of cutting through the cold of space.

Sampson had designed it, mainly as protection in the direst situations or to get them clear of a tractor web. The galaxy kept heading toward dark places. When a big plot involving an ambassador's plan to kill numerous individuals to refill the bone powder stores of the APU had been revealed four years prior, Emilio and Toni had been concerned about the safety of those they loved.

The easiest solution had been to equip *Gina* with a better form of defense, though this was the first time they were using it.

"You can't kill them." Zasha charged towards Dotti and the control panel. Sampson reached out, grabbing her by the arms, and she struggled against him. "This plan was so we wouldn't need to kill anyone."

Sampson held her fast. "You've never been a big fan of not killing."

"I am now. Life is not worth wasted. The pitch…" Zasha's eyes filled with tears and her voice trailed off.

"Is what we're all caught up in. These pups didn't care about our lives. You said it yourself, they were going to send us all to salvage and they know who we are. We can't risk everything, or their report being entered into the system." Sampson found himself unmoved, even by her tears. She'd chosen him and the crew but was still fighting for the enemy.

Bitter truths and the words burned like acid on his tongue, a painful numbness spreading into his limbs. He might be blackening his soul as Zasha had alluded to, but he'd sacrifice anything to keep his family safe. They would do the same for him, even if they didn't believe him capable enough of remaining in charge.

This will show them. Show her.

Everyone needed to see Sampson make the hard choices. The ones for the good of those under his care.

Lee stepped into the room, as Zasha sagged against him. He didn't miss Lee's frown at Zasha in his arms, a warning, and a reminder not to get caught up. Deep down he wouldn't regret getting a moment to hold her, even when they were at odds. *I truly am a bastard.*

The weapon fired. A riot of color exploded across the sky, red, orange, blue and purple flashed before their eyes. With the checkpoint on fire, it lost sustained orbit and crashed into an asteroid within seconds.

Sampson moved with a sagging but compliant Zasha toward two chairs behind Dottie. "Strap in, crew. We need to depart immediately."

Everyone else followed suit, securing themselves at the other stations around the bridge as the ship's slip drive powered up and they took off. It was a little more dangerous than normal with the absence of the trolling motor to navigate through the asteroid belt, but the explosion negated extreme caution, the need to remove any chance of getting caught in a concussive blast a priority.

Minutes ticked by and finally the slip drive slowed, the winding sound reverberating through the hull.

Gina's light flashed. "We are at a safe distance. Might I suggest we open fire from a similar gap in the future, Sampson?"

"Good idea." He didn't dare look at Zasha, who he'd left slumped and strapped in her chair.

"What next? Maybe another gunfight or let's blow a window out." This from Lee, who appeared eager, even with her doubt and sarcasm. He didn't appreciate the bullshit when the messes kept finding them and not by choice.

"We call the Smiths. They need to know about the pups. Those were Humans First members, weren't they, Zasha?" He finally put his gaze on her and tried not to let guilt swamp him.

Zasha nodded as she swiped angrily at the tears streaming down her cheeks. He wanted to believe she wept for human life in general, but a tiny bit of him suspected she had closer ties to those Humans First members. Doubt, a vicious lingering bitch, still whispered to him about her loyalties, even though she'd helped facilitate their escape.

Sampson moved towards the communications panel. "Right, so we let them know Humans First is behind this—let's be honest—and that they have members in the APU. Strange crap, but true."

"What about her?" Lee pointed at Zasha.

Zasha stared back at Lee defiantly with red-rimmed eyes. "I helped save you from those dead men, and you killed one without provocation, but you're worried about me?"

Lee shrugged and the motion of her shoulders sent her ponytail flying, hair whipping about.

Sampson held up his arms. He wanted a truce until he could learn more. "She helped us, Lee. Any effort matters. As for what next, we stick to the plan. Zasha comes with us to the moon as a bargaining chip or a way into negotiations with Humans First."

He didn't miss Lee's muttered, "For now."

Chapter Seven

Another epic fatching solar day came, and Zasha chose to spend it in the quarters assigned to her. She'd cried again, tears for dead assholes who'd probably cared very little for anything but themselves. Working so hard to save lives only to see them shattered because of paranoia ripped her nerves and sense of calm ragged.

Sure Sampson, the crew and Gina might have made it on a radar bulletin, but it wasn't like they weren't all listed as wanted by the APU already. Hell, if Zasha had given her real name, the same pups might have turned on her. The flash rewards for her capture were high last she checked, enough where even loyalty to a moral cause might take a back seat at getting paid. The right thing often failed in the face of a hungry stomach.

Then Lee had killed the dumb one. Zasha expected bullshit from Lee, a trained assassin who'd once been a special guard for the upper echelons of parliament. She had one way to answer any situation—with violence, knives and fists. Then Sampson had ordered Gina to fire on the pup ship.

It was fatching wrong.

He'd never acted like the type to end lives without reason, and his reasons yesterday had failed to read as honest. She'd cried for Sampson's inability to trust her and her plan. Cried for those lost, even if they were bad people.

We're all bad people when our lives are up for the taking. Another one of Jennifer's gems. How often had Zasha been the bad person? In the end the guild had turned on her.

Zasha snatched up the holo-screen from the bed. There were numerous communications the pups had shared with her. The dispatches had crisscrossed through the checkpoint as a way station for messages between the Humans First home base and the upper planets. The pups had stuff from Kascade and Darren. The words, the plans, made her question everything.

She'd been taught Humans First was about peace, not violence. That they only used violence in self-defense but tried to escape first. The holo-screen in front of her told a different story, one she didn't want to believe.

"They have food ready in the galley if you want any," Gina said, interrupting Zasha's musings.

"Thanks, but I'm not hungry." She flung herself back on the bed, lying against the pillows with one arm propped under her head.

"Are you sad that we killed those men?"

"Yes. They didn't deserve to die."

Gina's light turned green. Sampson had spent time telling her about Gina's different light colors and their meanings. "What's confusing, Gina?"

"You would let people live who were trying to kill others."

Zasha frowned. "I would have stopped them from killing, too."

"People often say they will do things, but I have seen where saying things and acting upon them doesn't always occur."

A harsh reality, which made Zasha question her own motives. She wanted happy endings for everyone, but at the same time if she functioned by the theory of karma, the ending the pups received was well deserved.

"It's not easy to always do what one wishes."

"Do you wish to talk more with Sampson? To apologize for those misdeeds of yours?"

Zasha lay back on the bed, punching her pillow. "More discussion seems pointless. He doesn't want to hear apologies, but I have no way to show him."

"Then would you like me to have Sampson come to your quarters to discuss what you discovered?"

Zasha almost cursed but stopped herself. The AI of this ship was too damn intelligent. "You could share it with him."

Gina's blue light let out a little hum, almost like a laugh. "Yes, I could, but this defeats the purpose of getting you two to spend time together. He holds too much emotion for you still and it bothers him."

So, the ship wanted them to play kiss and make up. Funny and a little embarrassing, since Zasha disliked having an audience to begin with. Yet, she appreciated the efforts by Gina, where her own lacked.

"Don't get your hopes too high."

"I won't. Sampson has been alerted. He will be here momentarily."

How does she do that? "And why won't he just communicate over the com system?"

"Because I told him it's much better to see this in person."

Zasha rolled her eyes and sat up, moving off the bed and toward the small bathroom. She straightened her hair, clothes, checked her breath.

Ridiculous.

Exactly how she was acting, but she wanted to try. With all the mess going on, the potential death, dismemberment...hell, nothing could be set in stone. She only had the opportunities in front of her. And after what she'd read on the holo-screen, she needed something to distract her.

I'm pissed at him.

And she loved him. *Sampson made the call he had to, right?* A call she would have made if her hand were forced.

Her door chimed.

"Come in."

Sampson stepped inside the room with confidence. That paired with his ruffled wave of ginger hair and the shadow of stubble along his chin and cheeks meant she had to stop herself from clenching her legs together.

"You wanted to see me." The door slid shut, effectively locking them in together, and she wanted to forget about business, about apologies. Somewhere amid this mess of his arrival, her brain had got more physical and less emotional.

Focus.

"Yes, the pups, before they got blasted to hell, shared some disturbing intel. Seems like the checkpoint served as a halfway stop between communications from Humans First on the moon to the uppers. There may be more sympathizers or members inside APU operations than even I had knowledge of. Hell, all this is fresh info to me and kind of scary."

She walked over to her bed, picked up the screen and brought it to Sampson, who met her halfway. Their fingers connected as the trade-off happened, and she still experienced the same tingle as she had before from the link. The basic connection sparked the memory of the kiss they'd shared, the opportunity for something, but she needed trust.

"There are communications to mercenaries too. Isn't this one your—?"

"Yes, my old mentor, Jennifer, the one who sent me on the Io mission." The one who'd tried to kill her, but Sampson was unaware of the murder part. He'd missed what had happened after Zasha had escaped after completing only half of her job on Io. She had been supposed to get the scientist's device as well, but had failed, because she couldn't betray Sampson all the way, not after he and the crew had saved her life.

Sampson kept reading, swiping his finger up the screen moving between the messages. "We need to stay alert. Who knows if these mercs are moving to intercept us or working to stop anyone coming for the kid?"

"Based on those, we know they at least have ships already through the checkpoint at the asteroid belt," Zasha added.

Gina's light hummed to life. "I have already started working on extrapolating trajectories from the checkpoint and plotting a fast course with minimal contact."

Of course she had. "Thanks, Gina."

The light dimmed, and Zasha shook her head.

"What?" Sampson asked, glancing up from the screen.

"I don't know why I bothered telling you. Gina is already ahead of the game."

Sampson went back to looking at the remaining messages. "Communication is still important. Gina doesn't read minds either. She may be five steps ahead, but it pays to have a conversation. I think of things she hasn't and vice versa."

"Yeah, but she'd never tell you otherwise, might hurt your feelings."

Sampson passed the screen back to her and chuckled. "Oh, right? I think Gina enjoys the entertainment I provide. Did you need anything else? I've been double checking Gina's systems all day to make sure those pups didn't screw with anything and I still have more work to do."

"You really care about this ship." Zasha tossed the holo-screen onto her bed and faced Sampson again. This time no toolboxes, tables or screens stood between them, only clothing and a little distance.

Distance I can close if I'm brave enough.

"Gina is my best friend." Sampson's conviction filled Zasha with a little jealousy.

She'd never had a best friend. Anyone she called friend seemed temporary. Even those at Humans First, while nice, weren't close to her.

Because what I touch draws violence. Karma.

"I don't think anyone has ever said that about a ship. Must be nice, a best friend who won't go running at a second's notice, leave you stranded or trade you for crinkle." *Or try to kill you.*

"Best friends are hard to come by. I'm thankful for mine."

They were silent, though like two drifting asteroids caught up in each other's gravity they moved closer together. Finally, the small gap disappeared.

"What are you doing all this for, Zasha? You could have left us with the pups. Gone back to your precious movement, and ditched." He stood right next to her, arms flat against his sides, and how she longed for him to touch her.

She bit her lip, her gaze trapped on his. His eyes were like deep pools, drawing her in and sucking her down. For once she didn't let the simple answer come out. This time she confessed the truth from deep within.

"Forgiveness from you, and maybe I want a shot at being the person you thought I was."

* * * *

Sampson let those words sink in, absorbed them like a black hole sucked in light. He wanted them to be real. All of this.

Sure, they had some serious shit to deal with, but why not relish a little moment? She'd chosen the crew, the ship. Shown him the holo-screen with the messages. Although Gina had already told him about them, Zasha bringing it up separately had to mean something.

She needs a ride to the moon.

He pushed the inkling away, the Lee-like voice of cynicism echoing possible threats in his head. He'd rather be present in the here and now. Guilt already assailed him for having blown up the checkpoint, ending those pups' lives. He'd needed to take action — they would have killed them.

To hear her not degrading him, making him second guess keeping her on board, like others often did... To hear her holding herself to some standard…a standard she thought he possessed…

Goddess, I don't have dick.

He reached for her, pulling her closer to him. Leaning down, he touched his forehead to hers. "What kind of person is that?"

"A good one," she replied. "One who helps people."

Then he leaned back to get a look at her eyes, to see her gold depths reflecting such warmth at him. "Humans First isn't helping."

Those irises flashed and maybe the words had been the wrong thing to say, but they needed to be said. Humans First were terrorists — the information she'd shown him on the holo-screen proved their true nature. At his core he needed assurance that she realized this too.

Then she frowned, a small ridge appearing between her brows. "Can we not fight? It seems that's all we do. Either fighting for our lives or fighting each other, and I don't want to anymore."

Sampson debated the idea. Fighting had become second nature after their shared past. They were destined to constantly wage war, based on their different interests and beliefs.

"What do you want, then?"

"You." She leaned in, attempting to initiate a kiss.

He pulled back. "What about the trust thing?"

"Do you trust me?"

With those golden eyes staring into his, the desire and want swirling like oceans of liquid gold? He could drown there, lost to faux riches in those pools. He'd say anything.

No. Yes.

The truth.

"I don't know."

Fatch.

He'd gone and said the wrong thing again, but damned if he'd speak falsely. Wanting her and believing in her were two different beasts. "If that's not enough —"

She pressed a single finger to his lips. "For the moment, I'm settling."

Then she kissed him. The heat between them spiked, hotter than the sun. He couldn't get close enough to her, grabbing her leg under the knee and hitching it around his waist.

He wanted her naked, on a bed and eager to have him. She licked his lips and he responded in kind, giving as much as she gave.

Pulling away, she sighed. "Your answer... I'm not sure it's enough."

He slowly let his hand on her thigh relax, releasing his hold on her, though his other hand still sat against her cheek. "We can stop then."

"I don't want you to regret this."

He decided to go with a line Emilio had recited a half-dozen times. "The only things I regret are the chances I don't take."

It shouldn't have worked. She should have slapped him, but instead she kissed him with more fervor.

"Then let's not waste another minute," she mumbled against his lips.

Her hands roamed freely over his chest, gripping muscle structures he hadn't possessed when they'd last been involved. No, her betrayal had brought a lot of changes to him, including the desire to be able to have more power over his body and be physically stronger.

"Like what you feel?" he asked, stepping away from her.

She quickly regained her balance and came toward him again. "Yes. What are you doing?"

"Strip, first." His eyes widened at his brashness.

Zasha let loose a wicked grin and reached for the buttons on her vest. She tossed it aside in seconds and moved on to her shirt. "Afraid I won't follow through?"

"No, this is about the last time we had close quarters. We were fumbling fools, desperate for fast fun, half naked and seeking quick release. I want to explore this time. To appreciate what's in front of me."

She shivered, and he prayed the reaction came from his words and not because outer space made the rooms on a ship colder.

Her breasts were exposed to the air, their dark nipples pebbled. "I appreciate a little foreplay. Though I tend to enjoy a quick, hard fuck all the same."

Sampson eased a hand down and flicked off his tool belt, letting it drop to the floor. Then he stroked the indentation of his hard cock against his pants. "I've had plenty of those. I want you to give me what I haven't had."

She speed-stripped out of her boots and pants and stood before him with only a barely there scrap of cloth covering her pussy.

Hefting her breasts in her hands, teasing the nipples between her index fingers and thumbs, she slowly came toward him.

His mouth hung to the floor, and he didn't care. She was the sexiest woman he'd ever seen, then and now.

"I want what I haven't had, too."

Her hands left her breasts, and he longed to take over with his mouth where her fingers had left off.

"Oh, what's that?" His voice sounded so far away, like an echo in an empty ship storage container.

She grabbed for his pants, working at his buttons, getting her hands inside.

Goddess to hell and back.

"You might kill me before I find out what you want," he said with a groan.

"I want to put my mouth on your cock, and at the same time I want your mouth on me."

Right as she finished speaking, she wrapped her palm around his hard length and stroked within the confined space.

He shuddered. "I'm happy to oblige, but I might not last if you keep talking dirty and handling me like this."

She tugged on his cock roughly and pre-cum came spilling out, wetness seeping into his smalls. "But you like me rough and ragged. I remember."

The last thing—praise the gods—he needed to be thinking about were memories. Not when he wanted to be lost in the present. And he wanted to be a better performer than those first times. In fact, he could be the best damn fuck she ever had.

Sure, she'd said so back then, but he'd barely got her to come.

I can do better.

He reached down and removed her hands from his pants. "Yes, but I want to please you more this time."

Wrapping her hands up in his, Sampson pressed a soft kiss to her lips and guided her towards the bed. She dug her heels in right before he was ready to lie down with her.

"You're wearing a lot of clothes and that doesn't please me."

Sampson glanced down and quickly began shedding what clothing remained. Screw all of it, including his smalls. In seconds he stood naked before her.

Then they were on the bed. It wasn't hard to pull her against him and fall backward, and she let out a little squeal of delight as they went.

"Where do you want me?" he asked, moving to massage her breasts, repeating the motions she'd conducted in front of him, though he ached to put each hard nipple in his mouth. To clamp his teeth on the tender flesh and hear her squeal.

"Stay here like this." Zasha lifted up and away from him, rotating her body so her legs straddled his head, her barely covered pussy right above his lips. Her salty scent filled his nostrils. She was wet. *For me.*

Then all focus fled as she touched him. First with her hand, stroking firm, her grip like a vise, but it didn't prepare him for her mouth.

No, this was a new experience. He'd hadn't been lying when he mentioned previous screws all being hard, fast and with as little connection as possible. Connection was a damn scary thing after having been hurt by someone who'd been this close. No, he'd spent himself with one or two women at most.

So, when her mouth enveloped his cock in warm, succulent heat he almost had an out-of-body experience, like being tased without the pain and all the pleasure. He lay stunned into silence and inaction as she worked her beautiful tongue up and down his shaft.

Then she moaned.

"Fatch me."

She blew a breath over the sensitive head of his cock and licked the pre-cum from the tip. "I love how responsive you are."

He frowned then growled, "Let's see if you're the same."

Instead of going nice and easy, he hooked his arms around her thighs and pulled her pussy right to his mouth. He licked over the fabric, loving how fast she'd soaked through the little scrap of cloth.

"Sampson." She said his name as a shiver wracked her body. This was what they did to each other and they were at the beginning.

"I shouldn't hear you speak if your mouth is full of cock. Show me how much you want me to keep going. Take it all."

She did, swallowing him whole, but he refused to relent and when she nipped at the top of his head, he bit through the string keeping her cloth covering in place and exposed all of her.

No way would he let her get out of this without hearing her scream.

Chapter Eight

Holy sweet fatching hell.

Sampson had definitely learned a few tricks and what he didn't know, he made up for in sheer determination. A lick here, a suck there then full-on attention to the little nub at the top of her pussy.

Zasha attempted to keep her movements on Sampson's cock deliberate and matching, but with his devastating tongue, he'd been right—focus was impossible.

She had remembered those first times too, and they were nothing like this. Moaning out loud, she redoubled her efforts, swallowing him whole until the tip reached the back of her throat—something she didn't enjoy doing for just anyone.

Enough to realize wanting to please Sampson, to have this connection him to, might be damn risky and a bit foolish.

Fatch.

Sampson chuckled against her clit, scraping his teeth over that sensitive part of her, and her damn legs trembled. Everything in her tensed at the repeated efforts he deployed as he took the time to learn her body, to enjoy and savor. He slowed down, moving away, brushing his lips against her feminine ones.

"You are drenched for me. And you smell like sex. I want to be inside you."

She smiled even while pumping his cock in and out of her mouth. Coming to a stop, she gently pulled off him, letting his dick pop out, relishing his length and girth, which was more than enough for her single hand. Sampson was not small. He never had been.

"But I'm not done yet." She leaned down again with every intent to finish the job, and he dove in as well.

This time she lost all hope of finishing him off. No, he chased away the memories of every quick screw she'd had. Even the slightly longer fucks melted away as he dialed in on her clit with precision until she bowed up and pushed her pussy against his mouth, grinding and begging for release.

"Please, Sampson. Please."

The cries seemed to inspire him to increase his pace, the ministrations almost unbearable. That was when she came, her legs seizing into position as release found her. A beautiful moment that was punctuated by his eager tongue lapping up every last drop, as if her cum was too precious to lose.

She sighed and fell against his body, and his rock-hard cock thumped against her cheek. "You win."

Sampson moved out from under her and rolled her onto her back. A slow perusal brought a smile to his lips, then he followed with his mouth on her breasts. She couldn't move, exhausted by her release. She had no clue if she could reach such heights a second time. They had tried for a two in a row, once upon a time, but hadn't gotten far. No, because we arrived at Io and departed to betray me.

Zasha shook her head. "I can't, Sampson."

He lifted his head, still teasing her other nipple with his fingers. A little pinch, and she jerked beneath him.

"If you really want to stop I will, but..." He trailed off as he leaned down and kissed her.

She tasted herself on his lips, the scent of her pussy in his stubble arousing her anew. She liked him smelling of her and eating her out as though she was some fatching Saturn delicacy, and she wanted more of what he offered. At least more than the stolen moments they'd shared before.

"Don't stop. Forget I said anything and take me there."

"Where?" He softly kissed her lips then slid between her thighs.

He paused, his cock head notched right at her entrance.

"To a place that makes me forget everything."

"As you request." And he drove home.

Karma curse her, he knew how to fuck. The way he swiveled his hips, elevated her ass off the bed for a new angle and whispered her name like an old Earth prayer drove her wild.

His dirty talk, speaking at all, was new. He'd been quieter, soft grunts and huffs when they'd coupled. Now he talked about how beautiful she was. How she looked like a space angel, born of nothing and ether.

The words weren't lost on her, but at some point, the sensations he built within set her off to a different plane. She stopped focusing on words and lived inside

her feelings, the emotions he evoked with all his efforts and how she wanted more. *Harder. Faster.*
Less verbal assault and more animal rutting.

"Fuck me harder. Stop talking." The demands she gave did not provoke him.

Sampson answered each one and continued at his unwavering pace until his balls slapped against her body, and a slick sheen of sweat covered both her and him. She wasn't cold, not with the heat they generated between them. Their search for the unattainable ramped up, for pure peace found at the end of a chemical reaction caused by physical pleasure.

That was what her mentor had called it, the one time they'd shared a bed, where they'd rubbed their clits against one another until pleasure had emerged.
Sometimes release is required. Any person will do.

Except with Sampson, it had always been more than a simple drive to find release. It had been this attraction of a primal nature. A fleeting touch, even a look, could bring her to this frenzied state.

"Fuck me!"

Sampson reached for her then, shifting to lift her off the bed, supporting her back so she could plunge down on his shaft as he rose to envelop his cock in her slick channel over and over. She screamed, he roared.

Then peace, sealed with a kiss.

Except, she kept moving, even as he tried to hold her still. She wanted every last vestige of his orgasm and he whimpered a little as she took it. She claimed his mouth one more time.

Silently proclaiming...*mine.*

* * * *

101

Sampson couldn't fall asleep. Not for the life of him. Not since Zasha and he had orgasmed at the same time, and she'd kissed him. The last kiss they'd shared had reached in and possessed him, like he'd been harvested heart and soul and bound to this woman who lay beside him, sleeping peacefully.

How can she sleep?

This wondrous feeling overpowered, overran any effort to pass out. Wasn't that a complaint Toni, Dottie, and Lee had shared over and over, how men would be the first ones out after a wild orgasm?

Here he lay ready to jump up and fix the ship, do a spacewalk...eat her delicious pussy out again?

A definite idea worth exploring. He eased the sheet back off them both, starting the slide downward, moving Zasha's legs apart. She'd tasted delicious, and he'd loved learning what made her squirm and moan.

Now, to put his newfound knowledge to the test...

"You should be asleep." Zasha's voice halted his movements.

"I can't. For some reason, my mind is on overdrive and either it's build something or fuck you again."

He lowered himself between her legs and could see she was fatching wet for him at the mere mention.

"Normally, I would say you need your rest, but you eat pussy like you were born to. So, by all means don't stop now."

Thirty solar minutes later, give or take, she had orgasmed again. He loved working so damn hard to make her come. The efforts made him like a superhuman or something equivalent, but the smile on his face proved unstoppable. *I made her scream my name.*

He climbed up her and kissed the tip of her nose. As he started to ease away, she wound her hands around his neck and pulled him in for a deep kiss.

"I love tasting myself on your tongue. It's addictive. Keep this up and you might find me handcuffing myself to your bed, so you'll never be rid of me."

Sampson moved back beside her, and took his own cock in hand, stroking it. She covered his hand with hers, stimulating his movements, and he sighed in pleasure. This was what he couldn't find anywhere else.

He groaned. "I don't see you wanting to play willing sex slave for the rest of your life."

"If you promise to use your mouth on me multiple times a day, I could be persuaded."

Of course, that was when she chose to straddle him and guide his cock into her silken heat. She was in control this time, and he let her use him to her heart's content. Even when he was near the end, she drew out his release, halting her rising motions, which pulled him out of her slowly, then plunging down fast. *Fatching insane.* When he finally came, she hopped off and licked up his cum.

"Do you want to taste?"

He nodded, lured in by the seductive pleasure in her golden gaze. She leaned in and kissed him, his release shared between them. *Naughty, filthy and fatching amazing.*

When she stopped kissing him, she rose from the bed and smiled. "Be right back."

She could have demanded he fuck her until he died and he'd have done it. Maybe he was the one who should handcuff himself to the bed.

Yeah, until she lies to you again.

The thought came like an engine error message on a calm space travel day. He didn't want negative ideas intruding on this night that had played out better than the majority of his fantasies.

When Zasha came back from the bathroom and joined him in bed, she coaxed his head onto her chest and stroked his hair. "Have I worn you out yet?"

He chuckled. "I don't know if you can."

"You're going to really make me work for rest time, aren't you? Give me ten minutes and I'll be ready." She continued stroking his hair and somehow it worked, calming him down along with the steady rhythm of her beating heart.

He closed his eyes but woke to the demons. The reminders of her betrayal, the explosion, the look in her eyes and the shrug of her shoulders. Then the message.

He jerked awake and sat up.

"What's wrong?" Another problem with Zasha — she'd always been a light sleeper.

"Nothing."

Her hand came to his shoulder, which brought an all-too-familiar zing that zipped through him. She did this to him, and he craved it as much as he had the first time. "Don't lie. Remember I'm trying to be better, but it helps when you're not hiding from me."

Sampson gave a sad smile. "I wish you'd never left the ship that day. Wished you'd decided to stay with us instead of finishing your job."

She nodded. "Yeah, would have been the smarter choice for sure."

"What do you mean?"

The answer prompted a whole new set of theories, worries. He'd spent the last eight years being angry, now he wondered if she'd been safe.

"My mentor, Jennifer…she turned out to be the one who set my ship on fire. She planted a bomb, wanted to get rid of me. Then she tried to double-cross me after I escaped Io, without the prize."

Anger curled in Sampson's chest, like the formation of a small star. "But she came to get you."

"Ironic, right? The entire time she'd also worked on planning my demise. The completion of the mission would have been a bonus, but I didn't take the case. I left it with Gina, for you." Zasha stroked his arm, her eyes focused on the far wall. "Maybe I should have gone with my gut then. The merc life for the long haul wasn't for me. Not being able to trust people is a serious problem I don't want to deal with every day for the rest of my life."

"Why didn't you come back?"

She laughed, a detracting half-hearted thing. "Would you have taken me back?"

Sampson gave the question consideration for a minute and he couldn't answer her honestly. Because back then he'd been hurt, angry, and given her everything only to have it tossed aside because she had lived by a mercenary code.

"I don't know, but you took a chance now. I'd like to think if you'd taken the chance then I might have agreed to it. I could have fallen right back into what we had knowing you chose me over the guild."

But she hasn't fully chosen you.

This was an accident of circumstance, of luck. She'd chosen Humans First, some other lost cause with issues around honesty and good ethics, before she'd been forced to share close quarters with him. Emilio and Toni had made her his responsibility back then since he'd chosen to save her. Like everyone else, she was around him in the here and now because she needed him, whether for physical release or to hitch a ride. Taking out the trust equation, he still didn't have someone there for him. *Just for me.* His chest tightened a bit, and he thumped his fist against the bed lightly.

She spread her hand across his pecs. "I should have. Seems I'm not good at making the right choices."

"Then you don't think this was the right choice?" He leaned in and pressed a kiss to her shoulder.

Seeking validation again.

Well, so what if I am? He needed to know she wanted this as much as he did. Sure, her actions spoke to desire, but words mattered more. Anyone could get caught up in the moment, in an animal-type urge to find release. Their physical attraction had obviously never wavered even after years of frustration and anger.

"Oh, this definitely was the right choice." She pulled his face to hers and kissed him in earnest. "I've never felt so right about this one thing. Though, I think Gina hoped for this?"

"What?" Sampson leaned back, one eyebrow raised. "I doubt that."

"Really? Because she couldn't wait to tell you I needed to talk when I said I wasn't coming to the galley for food. She made damn sure to invite you to my quarters straight away." Zasha grinned.

"Hell." Sampson would need to speak to Gina about meddling. Of course, she'd known how much he had cared about Zasha and how lonely he'd been. He never hid his true thoughts from her. "Then she knew what I needed, and I'll thank her in the morning."

In the morning...something he wouldn't worry about now. Not when Zasha's wandering fingers proved she was willing and ready for another round, and he could get lost in her soft skin and endless sweet sighs.

Chapter Nine

Sampson smiled. The smile stayed no matter what and his cheeks hurt from the ever-present grin.

"What the hell are you so happy about?" Doc asked. "We barely survived getting killed yesterday and today will probably result in nothing different."

Of course, he didn't have a ready answer at least not one he wanted to discuss with Doc. Sampson shrugged as he picked up his coffee mug and eyed the dark liquid within. "We're alive. Worth being happy about."

"Come on, Doc." Lee snuck up behind Sampson and slapped him on the shoulder. "Haven't you ever seen the face of a well-fucked man?"

Red heat blossomed over Sampson's cheeks as he force-swallowed a huge gulp of brew. *Leave it to Lee to make something private and enjoyable into a public, sordid affair.*

"If that's the case, it's his business, Lee," Doc grumbled as he grabbed two mugs of steaming coffee and headed towards the bridge.

Sampson kept his seat in the galley, pushing around the dried fruit on his plate. He had half a mind to tell Lee to leave him the fatch alone, but he didn't want to continue the conversation. He could tell Lee was angry with him for choosing to keep Zasha alive and he refused to regret his choice.

Not after last night.

"Lee, with us heading into potential hostile territory, I wanted to see if you would do an inventory of the munition stores." Gina's request provided a glimmer of relief since the assassin appeared hellbent on hanging around and glowering at him until they got into an argument.

Lee grabbed a mug and poured the hot water over the instant coffee granules. "Fine. I'll do it. Sampson, when I'm done—"

"I'll find you." He could avoid the fight for only so long before it came for him regardless. Might as well meet the situation head on, but he wanted a tiny reprieve.

Lee stomped out of the room, which left Sampson with the one person he did want to talk to. And she wasn't even flesh and blood.

"You can tell me. She's out of range." Her blue light buzzed around the room.

He grinned anew. "Gina, it was amazing. Zasha is amazing. I had the best time in forever. If dying of happiness existed, I wouldn't be talking to you right now."

Gina's light blinked. "I can tell. You're youthful again. Cares swept away. It's like me when I do a system defrag, fresh and new."

"Possibly. I couldn't make the comparison since I don't know what a defrag feels like." Though he damn well remembered what coming apart in Zasha did to him.

"It's like being completely taken apart and put back together, divided yet made whole again."

Yep, Zasha had invoked the same emotions in Sampson last night, over and over. "I should be exhausted."

"Are you glad I sent you to her quarters last night?"

Sampson swallowed the last of his coffee before answering, debating his word choice. "Gina, matchmaking isn't your strong suit."

"But I read those books you like. Old earth stories, filled with adventure and romance, men acting bravely, women falling for them."

"Gina." Sampson sighed. Maybe he should have kept those from her. "Those events aren't real. They're stories. Make-believe designed to make a person momentarily feel good. To entertain."

The green light appeared. "Why tell a story if it's not true? You always say stories imply actions to be taken, ways to behave."

Damn teaching an AI emotions and entertainment, morals and ethics is hard. This was where Sampson struggled, though he continued to work at the instruction because Gina needed this. She needed him to give her the push in the right direction, though he wasn't perfect either.

Or is it really you need her?

Ignoring the little niggling voice of dissent, he focused back on the point. "Regardless of the stories, and those things, Gina, you can't deliberately try to force people together."

"Even when I know they want one another?"

He groaned and stuffed a dried peach in his mouth. "How do you know we want each other?"

"Your heart rates increase when you are near each other. The dilation of your irises is affected and there is an internal temperature increase. Your bodies have a chemical reaction, meaning you are supposed to mate."

Usually, he wouldn't have been embarrassed to talk about this kind of stuff, but at the moment he didn't care to have his sexual desires examined so closely. "Can you tell me what you found out about all the messages Zasha had?"

"You are uncomfortable talking about your sexual attraction to the mercenary?"

"I want to quit focusing on sex. Doc was right, we need to concentrate on the potential problems we have headed our way."

Gina's light blinked in understanding, and guilt wormed its way into his chest. He should have talked more about Zasha and the state of things, but for some reason he wanted to keep her and their bedroom activities to himself. How she affected him too.

Because I'd do anything to keep her.

"Zasha's information appears accurate from what I can gather. The merc guild is working in tandem with Humans First. I am unable to discover anything among the information displaying any leverage the Humans First leader has over them. Meaning they are paid for, which means—"

"They can be bought."

"At the same time Humans First has multiple sources of funding. I have located accounts on the banking planet. Those feed multiple small groups across the uppers to retain information, safehouses, weapons and more."

"Let's take one problem at a time. My goal is not to take out Humans First but get the Smiths' son back alive. We need to call Loyda and Al."

"On it."

A small holo-screen emerged from the wall of the galley. Usually, Emilio and Toni made the calls. Here Sampson sat, in charge. *How the hell will I pull this off?*

"Can you send a message to them instead? I don't want to talk right now." Sampson rose from the chair and took his empty plate to the cleaning sink.

"Sampson, the message looks better coming from you."

He shrugged. "Maybe not. I mean they gave me three solar days. We've reached the deadline. They could already have a cruiser on its way to the moon. Stick to the facts, what we know, and ask for more time."

He finished washing the plate and put it in the drying rack, then made fresh cups of coffee for both himself and Zasha.

"Where are you going to go?"

Sampson stopped short of the door and turned back around. Zasha needed more for breakfast than coffee.

"I'm going to work on making sure you're in top shape. Let me know what their response is as soon as you receive it."

Then he set about assembling dried fruit and grains for his sleeping merc, things she probably hadn't tasted in years, but he wanted to share them with her. *Thanks to Eden.* Funny how she'd left him on her mission at Io but had facilitated the creation of the planet which provided the food she'd eat.

Gina's light blinked. "I talked with them."

Damn, he forgot how fast she worked.

"What did they say?"

Gina's voice, though typically monotone, had a distinct note of disapproval, though it might have been his own guilt. "They aren't happy, but they said they will hold off alerting the pups until they hear from you. They want daily updates and no more silence."

"Fine." It was the best he could muster without a smart-ass response he didn't want Gina remembering. "We'll get back to them daily."

"Also, they are concerned about the pups, and Loyda thinks a private squad of people she can trust might be better. I wanted to add I finished my extrapolations from last night's reports we got from the pups and there is a likelihood our current trajectory will put us in contact with a merc ship."

Sampson finished adding the fruit and granola to the bowl and shoved the container of granola against the counter a little more forcefully than usual. "Fatch. Load them to a holo-screen, and I'll look at it later. I take it there isn't an alternate route."

"Not a fast one."

"Then we keep moving and pray they're gone before we get there." He placed all the items on a tray, then exited the galley and went straight to Zasha's quarters. Gina might've called him out for where he was headed, but she remained silent instead.

She might have had more to say on the topic, but if the ship could sense his amorous reactions, then she could also tell when he didn't want to talk.

Gina's light blinked as he came to a halt outside Zasha's door. "The data is on Zasha's holo-screen. I'll leave you alone now."

"Thank you." He managed the response then took a deep, calming breath to expel the guilt taking over in his chest cavity again. Living in the real world with the mess awaiting him and the crew could wait a minute. He deserved a few more moments of a dream.

Walking into the room, he was surprised to find Zasha still asleep. She snoozed serenely, tiny snores ruffling the edge of her pillow, a side of her he'd never experienced. The joy of having this part of her, witnessing the moment and committing it to memory buoyed him up and helped push the last of the outside world away.

He slid the tray onto a small table near the door and approached slowly. Normally, he would expect her to jump up, on alert. Hell, her first time on the ship, she'd always woken before him.

Except now, she didn't budge. He sat on the bed, leaned over her and pressed a soft kiss to her lips. His effort rewarded as she eagerly responded to him a second later.

When he finally pulled back, she stretched beneath him and opened her eyes. "Good morning. How late is it?"

He grinned. "Not late at all, probably early. Who knows or cares? I brought you breakfast."

She leaned up and looked past him, eyes going wide as a star's corona as she jumped from the bed, the sheet falling away to reveal all her naked glory. He almost fell backward right there, his body viscerally reacting to the sight of her in the nude, pants tightening around his crotch, his cock ready for another party.

Her openness with him disarmed him with equal measure, and she looked so innocent as she skipped over to the table, an eager grin on her face.

"Coffee? Fruit?" She inspected everything and squealed. "This is almost as good as last night."

He'd sacrifice whatever to gain the reaction over and over, even angering a few people for another solar day.

"What's the word on travel? On the day?" Zasha asked right before she took a long sip of coffee.

"We're on the path to the moon with the possibility we might come across a merc ship. Gina is monitoring the situation closely, and I...need to spend the day running maintenance." *Like always.* Because outrunning trouble required a tip-top ship and drive, which Sampson had maintained for years. No one wanted to be around that crap, getting filthy with little reward, besides knowing the next time they needed to escape in a hurry they'd regret not having someone to ensure they were ready to run.

"More maintenance? Then I'd better hurry up and eat. Don't want to hold you up waiting around for me."

Sampson sat back, spreading his arms behind his head to enjoy the view. Better to let her down gently. "You don't have to hurry at all. Take your time, enjoy breakfast, a nice ion shower...relax before everything gets crazy."

He would have joined her if responsibilities weren't weighing on him.

She bit into a piece of peach and gave a smirk. "Oh, so laze around? Nope, I don't need pampering. Besides, I think we've spent enough time apart."

"Spend the day with me then, we can be together every second...until we get to the moon."

This was what he wanted, more than anything. Someone who sought to be around him simply because they *wanted* to. Not out of obligation, to even numbers or because of orders. A person genuinely seeking his company for the pleasure of conversation, closeness and companionship.

"I would be honored if you'd let me." She scampered off then, grabbing her clothing and disappearing into the bathroom.

Sampson basked in this glow and enthusiasm from her, wrapped himself in it as he lay back on the bed and stared at the ceiling. He'd make this day one to lodge in his memories for the rest of his life. No debating the possibilities of running into mercenaries or being at the whim of wicked people's evil plots. No, only her joy and enthusiasm for him sustained at length.

* * * *

Sampson spoiled her. Rotten. She could no longer joke about handcuffing herself to his bed. Freeze-dried fruit, granola, good foods constantly available. With a life like this, leaving his side would be a punishment.

He showed her the upgrades to Gina, the weapons and the system software that helped her hack security systems and other advancements of education, so the ship's AI constantly evolved.

Plus, he'd perfected the cloaking system. Gina could now change in seconds versus minutes as she had when Zasha had first come on the ship. Amid all the sharing, they conducted the maintenance checks with little interruption. At one point Gina alerted Sampson that Lee still wanted to speak with him. Zasha wanted to inquire about why, worried he'd take heat for spending so much time with her, but she kept silent and tried to quell the bit of sweet satisfaction coursing her veins when Sampson told Gina to let Lee know she could wait until he had time for her.

With all the work finished, Sampson encouraged her to trail him back to her room. He kissed her at the door and told her to get cleaned up and he'd be back. The way he'd dismissed going to his quarters bugged her a bit. It niggled at the back of her mind around the ever-present issue with his lack of trust. She'd hoped her encouragement through the day would have been enough to let her see this last little part of him, but she wouldn't push. Not when she had him back again, his talkative, enthusiastic self.

"I hope you're still hungry." Sampson uncovered both the trays he'd taken out of the galley while she had showered.

She shook her hair out, choosing to leave it down. After last night he seemed to like her hair this way, and she enjoyed pleasing him. "I'm starved, all the running around the ship. I'm surprised you haven't gotten some more help to upkeep Gina."

Sampson shook his head with a frown. "No, besides I can't trust people to know what to do."

"That's why you would train them." She snuck up behind him, wrapping her arms around his midsection, breathing in his scent of metal, coppery and sharp.

He chuckled a bit, attempting to pull away from her.

"Are you still ticklish?" She lightened her finger touch, but still kept a firm hold with her palms.

He squirmed. "Yes, and our food will be destroyed if you don't let me go."

His threat worked, and she released him, because if this meal matched breakfast, she couldn't wait. "What is it?"

Sampson stepped back and the plate before her beamed with a riot of color. Thick squares of orange, white, slices of green, small balls of different hues…she couldn't even name the things in front of her.

"Definitely not food cubes." She reached out for a small green ball and popped it into her mouth. One bite and heaven exploded over her tongue, sweet with a touch of sour. "Holy fatch, what is this?"

"They call it a grape."

Grapes were glorious. She picked up different items and had Sampson name them off until she knew what everything was called. Then she gobbled up even more. The tray was half-empty by the time she noticed Sampson wasn't eating.

"Do you want some? Don't let me eat all this by myself."

He shooed her away with a smile. "It's all for you. I'm still a little full from breakfast. I'll admit I don't have as much of an appetite anymore."

"You're too skinny. It wouldn't hurt to have some."

So, he did as prompted and grabbed a couple of cubes of cheese, some grapes and pear slices. "As you desire."

They ate their fill then she lay back on the on bed, leaning against him, amazed at her gluttonous behavior. "I'm so stuffed, I don't think I could move. Where did all this come from?"

"Eden."

The planet she'd helped create in a roundabout way. While he hadn't said it outright, Zasha remembered the contents of the case she'd left with him.

"How?"

"With gardens and flowering trees growing fruit galore. The planet has attracted biologists, ecologists and all sorts of scientists eager to encourage this new growth. They've been able to keep livestock as well and with everything so new and scarcely populated, they're working hard to ensure the land is properly farmed so the soil isn't drained of nutrients. Something Sweet said happened on old Earth, before the bomb and the alien threat."

She scoffed. "Aliens, the lie the APU made up. If Eden has all this, why hasn't Kascade talked to Sweet about a trade? Why hasn't Sweet talked to Kascade and the other moonie bases?"

The ceiling above was all bulkheads, painted to look more appealing, nothing fancy and yet the simple surface of gray and white hues helped her focus on the ideas swirling.

When Sampson remained silent, Zasha kept going. "I mean, not to sound selfish or greedy, but people are starving. A little food would go a long way to the moonies, even to those still struggling on Earth and Mars. Eden could level the playing field for the lowers."

Sampson sighed next to her. "I don't know anything about erasing the differences, but where were the moon folk when those on Callisto needed help, or the people like us? We were subjugated and indentured when the stoners possessed more technology than we could ever hope to have, technology to end suffering for families and prevent them from giving their kids away.

""You say not to sound selfish, but people are. Never happy with what they have, always wanting more. The blame can't be at Sweet's feet, not when he's responsible for dozens of people who abandoned their lives to start Eden."

"So, you're saying leave everyone to their own devices?" She rolled to face him, and he matched her actions.

They stared at each other, the fight looming. Tension in her body rose, along with the eagerness to prove her point.

"No, I'm saying if the moon folk had bothered to join up with the Martians, and those on Earth, they could have a fleet to rival the APU and the leverage to change their futures. This isn't one man not choosing to help — it's hundreds of thousands of people choosing not to help themselves."

She clenched her fists. "I disagree. It's easy to talk about the issues, to say the words, but action is harder when your belly is hungry, and you don't have a ship with weapons to offer protection."

Sampson reached for her fists, and she jerked back. "Zasha, I don't want to fight. Because this is an argument too big for the both of us."

She softened at his calm voice, even as moisture welled in her eyes. He was right, they might not see eye-to-eye on this, and she hated it. "Fine. I don't want to fight either."

It would put a damper on our almost perfect day.

Sampson gathered her up in his arms again and this time she went willingly. "Good, because I want you to tell me what you think of my upgrades to Gina and this big brain of mine."

She laughed. A loud, boisterous noise chasing away the anger of the previous moment. Sampson always worked this magic, coaxed out parts of her she'd locked away, including a youthful enthusiasm for life and adventure along with joy. Joy was something they didn't have enough of in the universe.

"Your brain is great, but I don't think you need me to stroke your ego."

Sampson winked at her. "Oh, I have something you can stroke."

This was new, Sampson and sexual innuendo. She'd never experienced the more sensual side of him until now.

"I'm sorry." Sampson tucked her hand inside his and pressed a kiss to the back of it. "I let the world intrude."

She shook her head. "No, I'm sorry. I get how Sweet and Eden are their own thing. I can't assume to know what's been done, what hasn't or why the hell I let the world at large get in between us. You were right—today is exactly what I needed. What I haven't had in so long…"

She trailed off, not drawing this out anymore and let the silence do the conveying for them. This little bit of time deserved to be about them before reality intruded all over again and potentially put them at opposite sides. If karma existed, then Zasha feared what it would take from her, what she'd lose.

In reality, the morbid side of her fully expected to have him dead in her arms at some point and it would be her fault. She shook her head.

"The world may have bigger issues, but for today and however long we have, I'd much rather focus on this." She lifted his hand to her lips and returned the kiss he gave.

Deep down, Sampson deserved so much better, but she'd said it before and would keep repeating to herself how she needed to try and be the person he saw her as. As someone important, like the way he stared at her now with stars in his gaze and devotion.

"I never thought I'd see this again."

He gave a small smirk and used his hold on her hand to tug her even closer against him. "What?"

"You regarding me as something precious and amazing."

Leaning back, he cupped her cheeks between his hands, then slowly lowered his lips to hers. No doubt he intended for it to be something soft and delicate, but she refused to submit. Instead, she forced the kiss deeper, wanting to swallow him up, whatever he'd give.

His scent, his taste...all of it. Thank goodness the tray of food was empty because she knocked the entire thing to the floor as she pushed him to his back and moved to straddle him.

Finally, she allowed him to break the kiss.

"Zasha." He breathed heavily, chest heaving. "But you are precious and amazing."

Chapter Ten

The sound started as little rain droplets, a once-forgotten sound Sampson remembered whenever they docked in the main city on Jupiter. The atmosphere on the largest planet tended to get stormy more often than not. Those storms filled his memories of his past...back when he'd been indentured, a slave to the Body Collection Service, and desired for his ability to finetune a slip drive to precision. Big Al had always said Sampson had brains none could match, almost as if he could speak to machines.

Then the sound got louder, a distress signal bursting into the ship. Zasha's ship on fire, her needing to be saved, and he had made the call. A decision no one else would have made to save the beautiful woman with the gold eyes.

The blaring was followed up with the explosion, gold and amber irises staring him down, twin knots of hair bundled on her head. Zasha had almost blown them all up. The shot to the scientist's head, the older man dead at Sampson's feet, blood oozing on the floor. Her grabbing the case and him going after her.

Sampson sat up, panting, Gina's light bar a mixture of colors igniting the room, the pulsating sound dissipating.

"Good, you're awake."

Sampson inspected Zasha, who continued to sleep. *How?*

"I programmed the signals to only impact your brainwaves."

Fatching hell. "You can do that?"

"Well, I've never tried it before, but I guess...I can." *New things, I'm learning how to do new things.* This type of growth should scare him, but he didn't have time to focus on the ramifications of her ever-evolving abilities right now.

"What's the problem?"

"We are almost to the moon, but there is an SOS coming from a ship. It's adrift and not more than a trolling burst away."

Zasha snuggled up against him, and Sampson couldn't help but lie down and let her tuck herself up next to his body. Her soft sigh sent a gust of warm air over his bare chest and he' recalled the state of post-coital bliss they'd shared a few solar hours earlier.

Damn.

"What do you want to do?" Gina's blue light came through crystal clear.

"Who's on duty?" Because he didn't want to deal with Lee. Not yet. He'd avoided her all day yesterday, planning to slip away after eating with Zasha to have a showdown with Lee, but things between them had gone further. Even amid the tense conversation, they'd found a way to resolve things and she hadn't wanted him to leave her side, though he dreaded Lee's ire.

"Dottie."

The tension in his frame eased. "Tell her I'll be there in five."

Gina's blue light extinguished with a fading, "Aye, aye."

Something she'd rarely said to him, although she spoke to Emilio that way. Her using a captain's response made him a bit more confident as he slid out of bed and got back into his clothes. He probably needed a fresh set and an ion shower, but this would do for the moment.

Zasha groaned, rolling onto her back as she stretched out over the bed. "Where are you going?"

"Got a SOS coming from a stranded ship." He slipped into his grav boots, cinching the straps tight.

She appeared fully alert now, turning on her side facing him, her gorgeous breasts exposed from the sheet. Those damn mounds with their erect nipples teased him, begging him to come back to bed. "What will you do?"

"Get to command and find out more."

"I'll join you," she replied, propelling out of bed at top speed.

He headed for the door and didn't stop to wait. "Take your time getting ready. I'm sure it's nothing."

A part of him knew damn well Gina wouldn't have alerted him for a random ship. This had something to do with Darren and the mercs. He could have waited, but he'd said five solar minutes and those were ticking down. The excuses rattled off in his brain, but he couldn't shake the fact that the reality they'd been running from had pointed a primed gun directly at their faces.

Sampson reached command in perfect time. "What do we have?"

"Darren's ship." This from Gina.

"It's dead in the water, probably a good twenty-minute trolling motor boost from the closest moon base docking area," Dottie added.

The holo-screen had multiple images of the ship clearly identified. It appeared to have taken some sort of beating, with a big hole in the starboard side.

"Hails?"

Dottie shook her head. "No luck. I've been trying for the last ten solar minutes, and nothing."

"Keep going. There has to be someone."

Gina's light blinked brightly. "Analysis indicates a lack of breathable air. The hole has no protection over it, but my scans show no presence of bodies in space."

Sampson snapped his fingers. "Then a force field is in place on the other side of the hole. Maybe there's extra shielding from a secure door."

The ideas were thin, spitballed in the hopes they didn't find the Smiths' kid no longer breathing.

"He's probably dead. All of them are." Zasha's voice sounded from behind him.

"We can't think like that. It's not productive or healthy. We need to have hope." Sampson said the words on autopilot because they were the right thing to say, but he'd stopped fully believing them a long time ago.

Zasha gave him a sad smile, one of pity. "I have hope for humanity in general, but in these situations, past experience weighs against us. The only way to get a true answer will be to go over there. Shuttle?"

Gina's light blinked. "Prepped and ready to go, whenever you are."

Sampson frowned, not sure who he was mad at — Zasha for debating whether the kid was alive or Gina for volunteering for an away ship venture. Not to mention Gina preparing the shuttle without consulting him.

"Who's going with me? Sampson?"

He schooled his frown, locking it away. They had a job he needed to finish and get paid for no matter what the end result might be, though he'd feel guilty if the kid were dead.

"Yes, let's get to the shuttle."

Their efforts to get secured in seats, detached from Gina and docked to the hole in Darren's ship seemed to drag on for more than a solar hour. When they finally achieved seal, effectively blocking the breach, Sampson was the first one sighing in relief.

"Do you think someone attached another vessel and cut their way in?" Zasha asked as they suited up.

Sampson shrugged into his suit, zipped it in place and secured his helmet. "No clue but based on the size of the hole, it's possible."

"Who would attack him though? Especially if he was bringing the kid back to Kascade."

The question only added to a number Sampson already had. This attack made no sense, stranding a ship out in the middle of nowhere. When the only bargaining chip remained on board — if the child was there or alive.

"I don't know, but we'd better find out. Ready?"

Zasha secured one of the two tool belts which were filled with a variety of items a body collector would use, along with other things. Some were of Sampson's own design. Even those not on death barges carried similar equipment for protection, if nothing else.

"I'll follow you," she replied.

He pressed the button to open the door, and they stepped through the hole. Artificial gravity was no longer in place, judging by the number of floating objects about the room. *Thank goodness for grav boots.*

One click, and they were secured, even if the ships were slowly spinning and caught in the limited gravity pull from the moon. Eventually, this ship would get too close to the mid-size rock and the orbits would collide.

That was a problem to be dealt with as soon as they'd explored the ship, especially if the stoners on the moon targeted the ship to prevent future issues. They were known for their surface-to-air lasers, though the bases only used them to break up potential celestial and manmade objects from colliding with the surface.

"We should move fast."

Zasha nodded. "Agree. Who knows when they might try to break this thing apart, especially if no one hails. Though, it's not a bad ship."

"If you overlook the big hole into space cut in its side."

They walked down the nearest corridor, a genuinely creepy experience. According to the suit readings, the ship was absent of power, lights and oxygen. The basic details digitally scrolled across the visor of his helmet, another upgrade he'd designed. Space suits didn't normally have built in holo-screens. *Until now.*

Zasha gasped. "There's a body ahead."

She pushed past him, headed straight for the prone figure, her movements awkward, like a slow-motion jog.

"Zasha, wait a minute."

"I can't... Need to know." She slowed grabbing for the body. Then sighed with a slow laugh. "Close."

"Anyone you know?"

"No, there are more bodies ahead. Based on clothing and gear, they're all mercs."

Sampson looked past Zasha, turning on his wrist light to illuminate the path before them. Multiple dead bodies in matching patchwork clothing of leather and other materials. Add in a wide assortment of guns, knives and other weapons attached to their persons and they'd stumbled on a pile of dead killers and each one with distinctive laser weapon burns, signs of a pup attack, which raised more questions.

"If they're aligned with Humans First, why are they dead?"

Zasha shrugged. "Your guess is as good as mine. We should push on."

Sampson pointed up ahead. "I'm reading a separate power source. It's still generating activity. Go for it, and I'll head to command."

Zasha grabbed his arm. "No, we stick together. No separation. Sure, all these folks are dead, but we have no clue if some of them are alive and in suits. No risks."

He reluctantly agreed and followed her, both of them winding their way through the ship, past the galley, the med bay with more dead bodies and finally coming to a room off the bridge.

Right past the door, green light illuminated the room.

"Is that a fatching —?"

"It is!" Zasha squealed and scrambled closer. Her pure excitement for the presence of this one machine shocked him when she'd been so determined not to have any hope before. "A stasis chamber. Sampson, the child...he's inside. The vitals say he's alive and asleep."

Sampson for some reason didn't experience the same enthusiasm about finding the kid, but he tried to muster some as he paged Gina. "Alert the crew. We found the Smiths' son. We're headed back to the shuttle — keep the weapons primed."

A crackle in his ears then Dottie's voice came in. "Better hurry, we've got targeting sighted on the busted merc vessel from three moon bases."

* * * *

Zasha had little empathy for the dead mercenaries strewn in the corridors of the ship, not when they would have probably killed the child if the Smiths didn't pay the ransom. Keeping the stasis chamber intact, she and Sampson worked together to return the kid to the shuttle.

The biggest concern still niggling at the back of her mind was Darren. She hadn't seen his dead body and with the warning from Dottie, there'd been no time to check command. Unanswered questions were as annoying as trying to move this stasis chamber around the dead bodies.

"Dottie, how much time?" Sampson asked.

A snap then crackle came through the helmet. "We don't know. Gina's working on it." Dottie's voice cut in and out.

Sampson let go of his hold on the chamber, moved around to the front and began the task of kicking bodies out of the way. They semi-floated, thanks to the lack of gravity, though the burn damage and exposure made them stick together. Zasha wanted to help but had to keep the stasis chamber moving forward every little inch they cleared.

"Don't contact them again. Let's just move," she hollered.

Sampson nodded, but she could tell by the furrow between his eyes that he hated not knowing what was happening. It was strange that Gina hadn't warned them…yet. Zasha trusted the AI enough to leave things be.

Once secure on the shuttle, door closed and the pressurization stable, she removed her helmet. "I think we should get him out of the pod."

The small ginger-haired child, not completely helpless but immobile, slept peacefully. If the dials and gauges hadn't said otherwise, she would have assumed he was dead.

"I don't recommend it. Best we let Doc take a look at the chamber, make sure there are no traps."

Zasha frowned, glancing at the spooky green glow from the chamber lighting. "They wouldn't booby trap a kid."

Sampson gave her a look, one that bothered her, as if she'd lost her intelligence somewhere. "I think they would if given the chance. Sorry, but the mercs and even Humans First wouldn't lose leverage unless they'd already taken precautions in the event of a rescue or were getting paid. You know this."

She did. Hell, she'd rigged a couple of traps in her own past, but for some reason she'd thrown caution to the wind after seeing the kid. *Maybe I am getting soft.*

"I hate seeing him like this." It was nothing to do with the fact that he looked a tiny bit like a miniature version of Sampson, and she daydreamed about how

Sampson's future children would possess similarities to the man himself.

Sampson opened up communication. "Gina, have Doc meet us at the door, as soon as we seal up."

"Aye, aye. He will be on standby. Is the child alive?"

Zasha spoke up before Sampson could. "Yes, intact and alive but in stasis. Sampson is concerned about traps."

"I'll put containment around you when you enter. To protect against the possibilities."

Living in this damn world made a person paranoid. What she wouldn't give for a life without constant fear.

"What about the bases targeting the ships?"

"Delayed for the moment," Gina replied. "I will update you once on board."

The words sent a fresh flutter of unease through Zasha's stomach. Ever since Sampson had woken her this morning, a restless, nervous energy had taken up residence inside her, filling her to the brim with the urge to move instead of standing still. *Movement in the face of uncertainty.*

They docked back to *Gina* without issue, and Doc stood there, suited up, right outside the shuttle door. They nodded at each other as the doors opened.

"Should we wear helmets? The traps?" Zasha's questions bubbled out of her, the nervous energy rapidly expanding.

Doc nodded. "There are extras right outside the medbay door. We'll put them on there."

They wheeled the chamber down the hall, around a corner and, as promised, three helmets awaited. Lee stood farther down the corridor watching...*always watching.*

She was probably a version of what Zasha could have become and, though she admired the woman, Zasha despised the constant ready-to-kill mode. She wanted to fight against her vengeful nature, not embrace it until there existed no difference between love and death.

Once inside the medbay, they got to work. Zasha helped where she could, scanning the chamber and providing tools.

After about fifteen minutes of visual and non-visual testing, Doc finally took a step back and sighed. "Appears there's at least one trap. It's a chemical aerosol. Looks like liquid nitrogen from the scan."

Sampson eyed Zasha, one eyebrow raised. "Good thing we exercised caution, or the kid would have been a frozen block."

Doc peered at his readings again. "And possibly us. There's enough in this tube underneath to douse a whole room, even take out a ship."

Zasha frowned. "Is that what happened to their ship? They fatched up placing the nitrogen and blew the side of the ship out?"

Doc bit on his lower lip as he worked the tools, crouching down beneath the chamber. "Eh, maybe. Accident re-creation is not my area of expertise. Zasha, come down here and be ready to catch this tube as soon as I finish unscrewing it. Sampson when I say go, press the hatch release and remove the kid. Fast."

Zasha moved into position, opposite Doc, her hands poised and steady, even with the thick-ass suit gloves. The tube itself was a glaring reminder reality had reached them. Being optimistic was fine, enthusiastic for life was good, but taking chances, urgent ones, could get someone killed.

Could have got this kid killed.

"Go!" Doc finished the last of his wrenching and the tube popped free.

Zasha grabbed it as she heard the chamber hatch hiss open, and Sampson moved in close. She didn't physically see the kid, but assumed Sampson had a hold of him when he stepped back.

Nothing happened. Appreciate that, Karma.

Zasha slowly stood up, thankful for her agility. "What do I do with this?"

Doc gently took it from her. "I'll store it away. Who knows when we might need the stuff? It can come in handy. Gina, a chemical hazard seal for this one."

He placed the tube in a box and Gina's light emitted a laser-like beam. *Holy hells.* This ship continued to wow her as it sealed the box.

"Pressurized and sealed, Doc. The room is now clear—you can remove your helmets. The baby needs your attention. His heartbeat is faint."

Doc and Zasha both scrambled over to Sampson, taking their helmets off as they went. Doc reached for the tools of his trade and discarded the engineer bits. Zasha stood there useless, wanting to help and not sure how.

Sampson's brow was furrowed again. His gaze on the child middled between apprehension and concern, with his hands awkwardly holding him.

The kid dangling there was a toddler, not younger than one but no older than three. *Around the age of my brother…before.*

"I'll take him." Zasha stretched out her hands. "You can go see what's up with the moonies."

"Here." Sampson handed him over without hesitation. "Sorry, Doc."

Doc shook his head and waved a hand towards the door. "Go, boy. We'll be here getting this handled. Zasha, bring the child to the table. Quickly."

Sampson left the room like a fire chased after him. It made her kind of sad to see him so bent out of shape and she failed to put a finger on the cause. Sure, Sampson had been one of the youngest in his family, ripped away as a young kid. While he'd spent most of his years growing up around adults, kids shouldn't have scared him.

He must have been worried about the ship or nine million other things.

"Zasha, hold Jace's head straight."

Jace...a perfect name for the little boy. She did as requested and stared down at the child's face between her hands. Her brother had possessed the same cherubic looks, like a little angel innocent and precious with baby fat still present. While Jace didn't have the same coloring, she got lost in those looks and even more lost when the small one's eyes fluttered open, revealing green irises.

A little Sampson lookalike, though his skin was a shade or two darker.

Jace opened his mouth, first for a whimper then a cry.

Zasha leaned in close. "Hush, little one. I know we aren't your parents, but we will have you back to them soon."

It took more than a few soothing words to calm the kid, who got progressively grumpier as the minutes ticked by.

Doc eventually administered a sedative. "We'll get a place for him to sleep ready, some food and things. Maybe even a bath."

"I can help." Zasha saw a chance here to right yet another wrong. Deep down, she couldn't take full responsibility for this one, but if she could stay close and ensure Jace's safety until they got him back to the Smiths, then she'd do it.

Doc nodded. "Aye, I'm sure but I'll manage this one for the moment. You better go see if they need any more expertise dealing with the moon and your people."

Her people…a big overstatement.

She had no people, except the ones she kept trying to tie herself to. The moonies she'd gotten to know were few and far between, though she had a knack for catching onto names and faces. Plus, Kascade needed to be dealt with, in some way. There were too many unanswered questions, with no one to pay for the kidnapping of Jace if Darren were dead. Except she had no clue to his whereabouts.

Might be why the ship got attacked.

"Fine, but if you need my help, let me know."

"I will," Doc stated, but he was already busying himself with steps for Jace's bath.

Zasha left and headed to the command deck. When she got there, Gina's voice could be heard loud and clear.

"The distress signal is now from one of the moon bases. Looks like they won't be getting rid of that other ship any time soon. They need help — something about an attack on Humans First. The other three bases have stood down. They don't deem the ship a threat yet and won't risk BCS and APU retaliation if there are bodies to collect."

No one else spoke, so Zasha did. "We need to help them. Answer the hail, let them know help is here."

"No, we don't need to do anything." Sampson offered this up, and Zasha's jaw dropped.

She would have expected it from Lee, who stood on the other side of the room looking at a holo-screen with disinterest. But Sampson, he always helped others.

He'd helped her. She'd fallen in love with him because of it...still loved him. *Damn it*. This wasn't normal.

Her open-jawed gaze appeared to have no effect as he looked at her and spoke again. "We have what we came to retrieve, the kid. The Smiths are waiting. I've communicated the survival of their son, and they want him back right away. We can forward the SOS to the APU."

Zasha cheeks got red, anger flushing her system. "APU? Like *they* would come. Not for the moon. Besides, what if they were the ones to attack? The laser fire on the other ship is pretty consistent."

Lee chuckled darkly. "You forget how much the APU loves moonie technology and the majority of it comes from the moon."

She shooed Lee's comment away with her hands. "Until now, no one has known the Humans First base was on the moon. You transmit a message saying as much to the APU and they might attack. You can't possibly tell me you're fine with killing innocent women, children, men and even elderly. People don't deserve death just because they believe in something different."

Lee took a step back, a physical and a mental one, judging by the shrug of her shoulders and the glance she leveled at Sampson.

"I await direction, Captain." Gina said.

Maybe Sampson should have been the one who answered, but he and Zasha spoke at the same time.

"Set course for Saturn."

"Tell the moon we are on our way." Zasha pivoted on one foot to face Sampson. His glare reignited with fury, similar to what she'd seen when they'd met again in the bar.

For all the frustration and acting as if she'd betrayed him, now he represented everything she despised about the mercs, selfish survival instinct damning anyone else in its way.

"We have to help those people, Sampson." This from Dottie.

Lee sighed. "Normally, I would disagree with Zasha on principle, but she's right. Innocents don't deserve death for thinking differently."

Sampson growled and stomped towards the corridor, heading in the direction of the personnel cabins. "Gina, answer the hail and set course for the moon."

Then he left, even as Gina's message of compliance echoed around them. Zasha stood, fighting against the temptation to chase after him. Because he wouldn't want the words she had to share, and she didn't want to disappoint him all over again. In the face of the real world, their differences mattered more than they had hoped.

Chapter Eleven

Sampson was a boy all over again as he stood in front of the mirror in his bathroom, splashing water on his face to clear away the soap from cleaning up. Not a full ion shower, but something to get the grime and muck off him after sweating away half his water content in that damn space suit.

Everyone, including Emilio and Toni, believed he enjoyed being dirty because he worked on slip drives and dealt with the inner workings of bone powder and whatever liquid it could combine with, which was often piss.

Since he'd been thrown into ship engineering at the tender age of ten, he hated it. Nothing beat clean skin, washed and dried. He'd suck it up when necessary, though grime on his face annoyed him the worst.

Scrubbing the latest away didn't change his mood, though. Normally, a good clean would wash away bad emotions, allow him to shove away the darkest parts of himself. This time he still scowled at his face in the mirror. He could have stood his ground, laid down the law as the acting captain, the person in charge, though all three women had overruled him, starting with Zasha.

She had waltzed in and taken over and anchored them to help a bunch of people who would probably be as likely to steal Gina or worse, kill them. These were the bastards who had hurt Gina the last time, anyway. He feared anyone with moon stoner knowledge getting near her.

Besides, what about the Smiths and Jace? Sampson had one job, to find the kid and return him. He'd done the first part, and the returning portion was equally important if he wanted to get paid, which should be the priority.

With more trouble looming on the horizon, the unknown reasons for the hole in Darren's ship and the attack on the stoner's base, the safest bet would be to get out of here. He slipped into a fresh shirt, grabbed his jacket and walked back out the door ready to take up his argument again before they landed.

Lee waited there, like a predator on the prowl, and near made him jump with her quiet, calm pose across the hallway. She worked a blade back and forth between her fingers, rocking left to right and over again, a near silent but deadly threat. "We are about to dock, or Gina's working on it."

Sampson frowned as he shrugged the jacket over his shoulders. "And you've changed your mind. So, let's tell her right now. She can hear us. We cut bait and run."

The assassin stayed quiet, her focus on the shimmering metal in her hand.

If he didn't expect her to pull back and stab him, Sampson would have grabbed the damn thing himself. "What's the problem?"

Lee twisted the knife around in her palm, weaving through her fingers like it was controlled by some other worldly force instead of precise human dexterity. "I haven't changed my mind, but those people who sent the SOS have gone radio silent. Gina can't get anyone to raise hail. She's talking to their AI in the system computer now."

"Talking to their AI? It's too dangerous." Sampson pivoted ready to charge forward and run to command, but Lee's stiff hold on his arm stopped him.

"Yeah, and she knows what she's doing. Gina's not dumb, Sampson—she's gotten a lot smarter than the last time those moonies fatched her up. Besides you can take a minute and talk to me. You stormed off earlier."

Sampson sighed, shrugging off Lee's arm. "Yeah, what about it?"

"So, you're pissed because we want to help people. I would say the not-helping part is more Zasha's usual line, not yours. Is this opposites day?"

"And it's not like members of this crew to dismiss the priority of the job, the part of the work that gets us paid," Sampson fired back, moving away from Lee. Though he trusted the older woman, like a big sister always watching out for him, he'd never really sparred with her like this. Sure, they traded barbs, but downright anger or frustration only came into play when Zasha was around.

"Well, I'm open to change. Open to possibilities. Besides, it's not like you'd listen to me anyway, since you brought the merc on board."

"I told you her presence was necessary," he growled back, fists clenched. Her questioning everything he did pissed him off.

"Don't get your slip drive jammed. I'm saying it seems like we're at odds again. I don't like it, but in this case helping is the right thing to do, and everyone but you agrees. You need to suck it up. This day isn't going your way, but it's business time. Emilio and Toni would have stepped in."

The words had a bit of a sobering effect on his angry mood. Emilio and Toni would have probably gotten involved, but... "Fine, consider it dropped. Let's join up with the rest and see where Gina is on docking."

Because the sooner we finish this, the better.

A few minutes later and Sampson was pissed all over again. "Where's Doc?"

Zasha didn't even look at him. No, she grinned down at the toddler strapped to her front. The kid probably could have gotten along on his own, but right now appeared perfectly happy to be locked up in a harness, waving his feet in the air.

"Doc is prepping a kit to go with him when we dock at the moon base. Wants to make sure he has all the supplies he may need." Zasha pulled at the straps of the harness on her shoulders. "He rigged this so anyone could keep the kid close. I told him I'd try it out."

Said kid, Jace, sat wide awake in his makeshift prison, all smiles with a small drop of drool and words too. "Where's Mama?"

"On Saturn, kid." Sampson rolled his eyes. He didn't like Zasha having the kid too close and was tempted to tell Lee to take him, but that wouldn't do any good either. Sampson listened to his gut and it told him Zasha wanted to ensure he didn't leave until she got done using this crew and Gina for whatever purpose she had in mind.

Fatching fantastic.

"Gina, where are we on docking?"

Dottie chimed in instead. "She's still deep in communication. It's a war of wills based on the coding screen. I can't communicate fast enough. Seems the AI on the moonie's' communication program believes Gina is a virus and is trying to lock her out."

Sampson glanced at the screen, the ones and zeros zooming by. "Dumb move."

Dottie chuckled. "Try reasoning with an AI program unable to evolve."

"I'm in." Gina's light blinked. "Reprogramming the docking doors now. We will land in the main docking bay. Dottie, please realign navigation so we will stop moving with the gravitational pull and shift to align with the door."

"Got it." Dottie's fingers flew across the boards in front of her, inputting the necessary calculations and releasing the locking mechanism.

How useless he was, standing here on the bridge waiting for Gina to do all this legwork. When they landed, Doc would be the one helping people. Even Zasha had extensive knowledge of the inside of this place.

"Why the hell do they need me?" he mumbled.

"To figure out what went wrong, of course."

His face went hot as he found Zasha standing next to him and a toothy-grinned Jace staring at him as well. "What?"

"You're the only one smart enough to zoom through those computers, next to Gina. I'm sure after what happened the last time she visited the moon that you don't want her connected too long?"

He nodded and looked back at the screens, watching the angles of their approach. "No, I don't."

His stance got stiff and awkward. He was horrified how fast she voiced his inner thoughts, like some damn mind reader from old Earth fairy tales.

Or I'm super easy to read.

Gina bathed them all in a bright burst of blue light. "We are docking in forty-five seconds. Please get seated and strap in."

Everyone scrambled to the various seats around the room. Once locked in, Sampson watched Zasha feed Jace a cracker, then a food cube and for a split moment he daydreamed about what it would be like to live on this ship with her, permanently…to have children. She appeared enthusiastic with Jace and not awkward or uncomfortable. He would have second-guessed her ability to nurture until now.

Zasha glanced at him as the ship began to shimmy, slowly moving into the sheltered docking area of the moon base labeled with a giant number four on the door. They shared a moment, eyes locked on each other, and she gave a small smile.

He'd dreamed of this before, but the dream lay steeped in a bunch of expectations she would never meet. Judging by her quick rush of anger at his preferences for not heading to the moon, she held him to standards in her mind as well. The young man she'd known before had gotten lost the minute she'd blown up the building he'd been in on Io. He'd tried to tell her, to get her to see him in the present, but somehow he'd gotten elevated to some self-sacrificing status in her mind.

"Docking secure. We are fully landed, and bay doors are closed. Oxygen is in place and the air breathable. Suits are not needed."

"Life signs, Gina?" They needed to know what they were walking into.

"Minimal ones. It appears the population for this facility is about a quarter of its normal estimated size."

"This facility?" Sampson freed himself from the seat and jogged over to the coding screen.

Zasha unsnapped her belts and followed him. "Yeah, there are four facilities on the moon now. Each housing a certain amount of people. Got to be too many for one place and over the last eight years more have sought refuge. Could have been some folks didn't like having to share everything they got from sales with everyone else. There's definitely some political dynamics, though I haven't gotten involved enough to be knowledgeable on the topic."

Sampson frowned. "Not good. This could be warring factions then attacking each other. Dumb stoners."

Zasha bumped him on the arm with her fist and little Jace mimicked her actions. "Quit calling them by that stereotype. You make it seem like they're druggies and they aren't. Sure, some use cannabis for recreational use and expanding their mind, but not everyone is into those things. Some are researching it for its medicinal properties."

"It's a term." Sampson rubbed at the spot she'd tagged. Although tiny, she packed a punch.

"They have a new one, moonies. People from the moon, please quit limiting them. As for warring factions…no, not possible. They may not like each other in some ways, but moonies don't do war. They don't have weapons in the traditional sense." Zasha approached Dottie, who took control of Jace's harness and hauled the kid away.

A bit of relief washed over him at the idea the kid would stay on Gina. He would be safe here within these walls, instead of out in the thick of things with the rest of them.

"If they build tech, they can make weapons. Malware nearly killed Gina." Sampson had sorted her out over days, though long-term work took years. These moonies could do a lot with a little, and he'd experienced it firsthand.

"The general population is listed as fifty people." Gina commented.

Sampson headed out towards the main hatch at the back of the ship, with Lee and Zasha flanking him. "Those numbers the same at all the other facilities?"

Gina's light blinked. "Yes, roughly the same. I don't detect weapons present in the landing bay."

Zasha and Lee kept up with him, and they made it to the main loading area in record time, near jogging toward the end. For some reason the closer they got, the more a sense of urgency rose, along with the beginning tendrils of fear coursing through him. Whatever was out there wasn't good.

Doc met them at the hatchway, a pack strapped to him and another in his hands. He tossed it to Zasha.

"I'll take her with me to help any wounded. A familiar face for the injured."

Zasha nodded. "Yes, this is the only base Humans First operated out of. I know almost everyone who lived here."

"Great, then Lee and I will try to ensure the area is secure and find out who was behind the attack. We catch anyone we'll let you know." Sampson double checked his belt, he still wore all the tools from the shuttle trip earlier with some added extras.

He moved to press the release button for the door then paused. "Gina, do not engage with the communications AI anymore. If someone is messing with these people, they could easily use your connection as a backdoor into your systems."

Gina's light blinked and let out a low tone of acknowledgment, already moved to radio silent, though her lack of response made him wonder if she experienced any sort of anger towards him.

Can she be angry?

The door opened and he stepped out, unprepared for the cries of wounded people, the scent of burnt flesh and dead bodies littered across the room like trash.

* * * *

Zasha wasn't sure what she'd expected, but injured, dying or dead folk had never factored in. The moon represented a safe haven for people like her, more than any other place she'd ever lived. Sure, every place was a target, but she'd never expected such violence to touch this place. They'd walked into the aftermath of a massacre.

The cries, young and old, the charred bodies…tears sprang in her eyes, and she wanted to be everywhere at once.

She glimpsed Lee and Sampson take off, without a second glance at the upstretched arms seeking assistance. They were focused, near damn unfeeling in the way they dodged people with begging hands grabbing for their legs.

"Zasha!" Doc's voice got her attention.

"What?"

Doc motioned to a woman who had her hand up, waving weakly. "See what's wrong with her. Start there and work your way around the room. Categorize everyone and what their injuries are. Leave the dead. We'll get them later."

Triage...a term she'd heard many a time when working with the mercenary guild. The doctor there operated the same way, doling out who got treatment based on the extent of their injuries and the time the wound would take to heal.

She made her way to the woman Doc had pointed at, noticing the burn marks on her shoulder and abdomen. "Who did this to you?"

She needed to triage, but what better way to help than to identify the culprits? The burns themselves appeared laser influenced. Laser weapons were used by the pups—no one else could afford them or had access. APU wanted their soldiers to have the best and they ensured it.

The woman let out a little cough. "Pups...they came in a ship. We weren't able to do anything. They moved most of us here...then...no oxygen."

Of course, stuck to the floors with pingers. She saw them now, could make out the little blinking red bulb tagged to a piece of each moonie's clothing. Zasha moved to release the magnetic seal with the simple press of a button. These were tools of the BCS, not typically used by pups. *Curious.*

When those launch bay doors had opened each time, the moonies in the bay fell victim to a lack of oxygen. How many had Gina accidently killed by landing here?

Zasha wondered if the SOS had been triggered on purpose.

Zasha reached into the satchel for the sealer, a little hand-held device meant to seal open wounds, stop bleeding and half a dozen other uses. She shored up the woman's injuries and gave her an immune boost shot. A glance inside her pack showed her the Doc had tossed in dozens of them. It would keep the woman from getting an infection and help her body recover faster.

"I've got to help others, but this should work. Lay here and rest."

The woman gripped Zasha's hand. "Thank you and bless the movement."

She pried herself loose from the other woman's grip and continued her rounds. Doc had already made it through three people in the time it had taken her to deal with one, though he appeared to be moving to those with the worst injuries.

Zasha abandoned the idea of triage after helping the second injury, and each person she stopped next to shared knowledge of the pups, the evil the APU had sent to kill them. Some of these were members of Humans First, while others were innocents who happened to live in the same facility.

The cries of pain and agony still echoed through the room, prompting her to move faster, to begin cataloging those who were injured more severely for Doc's expertise and a separate list for herself. *I can do this. I can save them.*

After getting to the last one on her side of the landing bay, she moved over to Doc. "I have the list, but we have to move quicker. People are hurt—some of these folks may not make it."

Doc sighed and leaned back from his crouched position. The small child beneath him, slept peacefully as he finished setting the child's leg. "I'm only one man, Zasha. An older one at that, and I will work as fast as I can."

"It's the Smiths' fault. They couldn't wait for us. This is APU. Every person who can speak is saying the same thing. Crying out against the APU for deploying against them when they had no way to defend themselves."

Doc let out a heavy sigh and went back to work, wrapping the child's injury. "Zasha, don't rush to conclusions. Anyone can storm in with APU gear and weapons. If Humans First was able to infiltrate the uppers so easily, then this could also be mercenaries hired by your group who were upset because they didn't get paid."

The miracles of modern technology allowed moonies to repair bones with simple tools and diagnose illness with a simple wave of a wand, yet they couldn't protect themselves from soldiers with laser guns.

She shook her head, tears flowing freely. "Humans First is peaceful. These people didn't deserve this."

Standing there, her fists clenching the list of names, pissed beyond belief and unable to do anything but keep moving or cry her eyes out, she wanted to scream.

"No one ever deserves it, but it happens all the same." Doc grabbed his bag and moved to the next person. "I say we quit worrying about placing blame. Let Sampson and Lee uncover what they can from the main computer and help me save as many of these people as possible."

She nodded her agreement, grudgingly, picking up supplies from Doc's main kit before she moved on to help others. Though the evidence lay dispersed around them as plain as day.

Chapter Twelve

Sampson spent hours poring over the surveillance photos, the ship logs and all the communications that had come in and out of the moon base. Everything he viewed only steadied his resolve against Humans First and Kascade, the leader. Communications addressed to this supposed fine figure of a man were the worst and the most damning. The evidence before Sampson sent the chase for this murderous bastard off-world and towards Mars.

The last place anyone should go.

"Sampson, are you still in the main ops room?" Doc's voice came over com system.

"Yeah, I'm here. Do you need something? More supplies?"

Doc waited a minute then his voice echoed, "No, I'll come to you."

While Sampson waited, he continued the work he'd been doing for hours, copying files and backing up systems in the hopes someone could be brought to justice for this useless slaughter. An attack designed to make the APU look bad, to make the Smiths look like power-hungry operatives, instead of parents desperately searching for their child.

He had even more proof from the earlier communications regarding Humans First posing as APU soldiers, how they'd hijacked weapons from the same checkpoint Sampson and the crew had come through with Gina in order to make this look as awful as possible.

Who does that?

"Who does what?" Doc asked as he stepped into the control room.

Sampson shook his head and glanced back at the older man, sweat on his brow, blood staining his clothing. Doc had worked non-stop, not taking a moment off. None of them had, and a good thing, because the possibility of a BCS clean-up crew wasn't out of the realm of consideration.

"I doubt they're coming back at all."

Sampson needed to keep his thoughts to himself. "Yeah, this doesn't look good. I'm seeing evidence Humans First is behind this."

"I expected as much. APU would never conduct an operation in this fashion."

And Doc would know. He'd told a few stories about his days before BCS, as a medic in the APU military branches. He was familiar with the processes, how they worked, the bullshit they put people through.

"What gave it away?"

Doc sighed and crossed his arms. "There would be no survivors and if there were, they would already be en route to Jupiter to the indenture sign-up stations or worse, the jail. No way would free bodies be left, and a

BCS barge is typically dispatched by the time APU starts an operation. They should have been here before we got here and harvesting away. Often the crews are paid a bit extra on the trip if they ensure no one is left alive."

Sampson did his best to keep his focus, to not gag at the image, though his stomach aired its grievances with a grumble. "What's going on down there?"

"We've patched up most of everyone we can. The dead need to be moved, and we need to decide what to do with them. It's something where we could call BCS, but they don't have jurisdiction here. Dottie suggested we radio the other compounds and ask what the protocol is for other bases."

Sampson nodded his agreement. "Seems perfectly fair, and I don't feel like giving the BCS any more bodies today."

"All right and last thing... Zasha, she's not holding up well. Everyone keeps telling her how the APU attacked, and she's accepting the words at face value."

"Did you tell her what you told me?"

Doc shook his head. "She won't listen, even after I tried to direct her focus to the matter at hand. Appears she's close with these folks. Regardless, we need to watch her."

"Did you hear that, Gina?"

"Aye, aye, Captain."

Since Sampson had taken over in ops, he had been able to clear the computer of any possible threats and silence the idiot AI running communications. After all the safeguarding, he had let Gina back in. Sure, he could scour the information himself, but Gina was faster and more efficient. "Find anything?"

Gina let out a chuckle.

"Yes, terabytes. From technology they haven't shared with anyone to Kascade's private files. Did you know this compound is developing synthetic humans?"

Sampson swiped on a highlight file that Gina popped up on the main screen. "We can talk about the fascinating technology stuff later. We need to know what Kascade is going to do present time. Do we have to worry about additional attacks on the moon?"

Honestly, he couldn't care less about Kascade or Humans First's endgame, but he did want to keep his crew safe, including Jace. *Without the kid I don't get paid.*

"Kascade partnered with the mercenary guild to learn about some reverse infiltration tactics, and they deployed those here. Honestly, I'm surprised Zasha didn't recognize these herself, since she partook in multiple merc missions. She may have been recruited by Humans First originally because she possessed this knowledge."

Fear swamped Sampson's gut, fresh and hot, like a sour mess of bad food cubes. She might have been using their crew as a means to an end all along, though it didn't match up with her eagerness to save Jace.

Unless Darren had messed up.

"Where is Zasha now?"

Doc piped up. "Helping move the injured out of the shuttle bay and into more comforting quarters. Lee is assisting."

They needed to do more research, get to the bottom of this, before Sampson could confront her. The last thing he wanted to be reminded of was how she'd used him before. To think she'd used him again hurt worse.

Except she wants to be with me when no one else ever does.

At the very least, he could rely on her desire to prioritize him, enjoy time with him. Though loving him could easily be overridden by her determination to fulfill a role with Humans First.

"I'm headed back to help them. Do you want me to send her up?"

Sampson shook his head. "Not yet. Gina and I will keep working. I'll message you if I need to talk to her."

Doc left and once he'd officially departed, Sampson spoke to the room, to Gina. "What if she caught the ship because we were her only way out? This whole ploy for Jace and caring about the people here could be another way to ensure she gets some money out of this deal. A little extra."

"You speak from a place of fear and mistrust. I see no proof she's playing us false."

Sampson chuckled. "Yeah, but she's a good liar."

"She makes you happy and cares about what you think. I can't see her betraying these people. You haven't been watching her move around the shuttle bay. She is devastated by what has happened here and haven't you said before grief can do strange things to people?"

Sampson wanted to believe, longed to put faith in Gina's words, but desperately wanting something didn't make it real. He needed some way to prove her intentions to himself, even as he warred within his own mind over whether she cared for him not, whether their feelings for each other meant more than the moonies. *If we mean more than the flash she could get from the kid.*

Sampson started the download for the last of the records. "I'm not as confident as you, Gina."

"Analyzing the situation with logic and facts, it's evident she cares about you, and I don't think she would betray you. At least not for the reasons you believe."

His skin prickled with fresh fear.

What reason would make her?

* * * *

"There's probably only three or four left." Zasha offered the information to Lee and Doc as they headed back towards the landing bay.

Some of the main areas, including the galley cafeteria and the main lounge, had been easily converted with as many cots as they could find for the injured. Those who weren't so badly off helped Zasha, Lee and Doc.

But no matter the number of people helping, the job was long, tedious and exhausting. Outside of her rage and fatigue, she missed the moments with Sampson, alone in her quarters, shut out from the outside world and wrapped up in each other.

A fairy tale dream…one she'd trade a lot for again.

"Zasha," a weak feminine voice called out to her as she passed through the rows of cots. The stench of burnt flesh still scented the air, even after Lee had confirmed the vents for the air systems were functioning normally.

Zasha couldn't clear the smell from her nostrils. Turning on her heel, she searched for the source of the voice.

A hand stuck up in the air and waved weakly. "Zasha."

She moved towards the hand, and its attached blackened arm. Reaching for the open palm, Zasha gently encased it with her gloved one. They'd kept gloves on, for precautionary measures. With all this illness, a small cut on her hands could prove fatal. She'd seen the horror before.

She recognized the woman's face instantly. "Terry, what are you doing here?"

The woman offered a pitiful smile mixed with a grimace as her skin pulled tight. The side of her neck was bandaged where the worst of the bleeding had been, though her arm had taken a chunk of the damage.

APU bastards.

"Hi, Zasha. I'm here because...he left me." Terry worked alongside Kascade as one of his analysts. She crunched numbers, information and data. If there was anyone outside his pair of right hands who knew what was happening, it would be her.

"What do you mean he left you? He was obviously escaping the APU, he had to leave...to keep the movement alive."

Terry nodded vehemently. "Right...think positive, think light, believe trust."

They recited the mantra again together, and Zasha embraced the false sense of peace the words gave.

Terry swallowed hard. "I didn't make it in time. He got out of here before the APU could silence us all. They won't get a chance to stop him, and I know where he went."

"Where?" Zasha crouched down closer to her.

She wanted to know out of curiosity and so she could track him down. What kind of leader left his people to die?

The kind who are out for themselves.

Her anger morphed with each passing hour, trying to seek out sense in a universe where none existed. In her eyes, Kascade was a coward and potentially worse.

"He's on Mars. He plans to negotiate with the APU there and has evidence of the unprovoked attacks. Victory and justice for the lowers will still be ours. We can win."

"How?" Zasha wanted the whole plan, from beginning to end, because somewhere things had gone wrong with the child kidnapping, the mercs and this attack.

Terry shook her head. "I don't know. I know he expected you to return, and he planned to tell you things. He talked about what a great organization you and Darren were serving. How you would return with the tools we needed to finish our mission. You may have come a bit too late, but Darren...we saw him leaving with Kascade."

She let go of Terry's hand. "Darren was here? When did he get here?"

Terry tried to shrug, and the effort cost her a moan of pain. "I don't know. I never saw him arrive."

Zasha embraced Terry's hand once more and gently squeezed. "Thank you, Terry. I will put this information to good use."

What good use?

Darren had made it to the base, but when and how? Kascade had expected her return. He had good things to say about her, and none of those revolved around how she'd betrayed Darren and would have stopped him from taking Jace. Somehow, she hadn't reached the top of their most wanted list. The Humans First members she'd seen today still considered her one of them.

The concerning part, even more than Kascade being on Mars, was how he'd left hours before. Before Gina had arrived to find the merc ship with the hole, before the APU had attacked… *As if this were planned.*

Stewing on this information, she went back to the landing bay and helped move the last of the injured.

Once they'd finished, the bay remained littered with the dead. Normally, in the uppers, the BCS would be deployed to pick up the bodies and process them. Harvest the bones and melt the rest away. The bones were burnt down to the carbon powder used to power any and all ships.

Now, as she gazed at the pile and her righteous fury spiked her temperature all over again, she wanted to burn them here and now so the BCS, the APU and anyone else who wanted to exploit them couldn't get them.

"What are we doing with them?"

In all the months she been on the moon, she still had no clue how they disposed of those who passed. Most people lived decent lives — at least she hadn't experienced death since moving to this hunk of rock. *Until now.*

"Sampson has put a call out to the other compounds to find out what is traditionally done."

Zasha's heart swelled at Lee's announcement. Another reminder her of how good he was. He could have thrown the bodies into space for collection, taken them for sale or harvest, because those things were enterprising. Gold leaves rained down on those who turned over dead bodies. How often had she'd seen mercs make unnecessary kills to get an extra round of crinkle to drop in the clubs and houses on Callisto?

Sampson's voice came out of the intercom, but the connection wasn't clear. Lee and Doc moved closer to the box on the wall and Zasha followed.

She reached them in time to catch the last part of Sampson's message.

"They say to move them down to the below levels. There is a processing room there and we are to dispose of them." Sampson didn't sound surprised. His words were simply stated with no emotion.

Zasha gasped. "What are you saying?"

"I'm saying, according to the other bases, the dead are not given any special treatment. They are processed like bodies across the galaxy and the powder is put into stores which the moonies sell as needed to ships passing by or trade to the BCS for supplies."

Tears arose anew in her eyes, and she shook her head, angrily willing them away. "No, we can't."

"If we don't, the other compounds will retrieve the bodies for themselves. Each group is independent of the others, and with so many injured here, they'll need the potential flash the powder can get them. You want to be the one to tell those people you swore to help why they can't get extra antibiotics or food cubes?"

Fatch it to hell and back.

This wasn't the plan, not here where they prized human life and the right to choose what happened to your remains after death. There were no good choices, no good solutions. Every step she took meant another inch into a darker hole and she didn't know where to direct the force of the explosion brewing within her. Sampson, the other compounds, the APU, Kascade...

The pain in her chest hurt the way it had when she'd lost her brother. The same as when she'd run from Sampson and the betrayal in his eyes.

"Let's get started then." This from Lee, who dragged over a big cart. "I think we can manage two at a time.

Maybe about six trips, give or take. Unless Sampson wants to get down here to help."

"Do you think they know?" Zasha posed the question openly to anyone willing to answer.

A hand patted her shoulder, and the tears welled without effort. She leaned into the connection from Doc, who spoke softly. "It's most likely. We don't have to involve the moonies if you don't want. It can be us alone, in case they aren't aware."

"No, if they know, we'll need all the help we can get." She couldn't swipe at her cheeks or eyes, so she blinked a couple times real fast. "Let's get this done."

The only way to survive is to soldier on, right? Her mentor would have said the same. No sense in crying over people who wouldn't care if she were alive or dead. She wouldn't shed any more tears for now.

Chapter Thirteen

Nearly a solar day later, and Sampson was ready to depart. They'd fixed up what they could, made sure there were people to care for the injured and assured the other compounds that Moonie base four was fine and productive. Because the other compounds were all too eager to send people over to find out what had happened. Zasha and another moonie, Rosh, warned Sampson to be cautious as the compounds were known to be potentially cannibalistic at the first sign of weakness.

A horrible way to live.

Back on ship, Sampson managed the communications to Al and Loyda about Jace. They were happy to hear once more how their son fared but were eager to meet up and also, less than impressed Sampson had allowed Gina to break into some humanitarian-geared mission. The Smiths were already en route.

"I don't disagree the compound needed assistance, but the APU —"

"Isn't trusted here," Sampson supplied as he picked at dirt under his fingernail to avoid Al's gaze.

"Fine." Al's reluctant tone got Sampson's attention.

The red-haired man could have easily been his older sibling, though Al's bulk surpassed Sampson like a gas giant next to an asteroid. Loyda stroked her husband's shoulder, which in turn obviously caused this intimidating ex-body barge captain to alter his next words.

"When can you meet us?"

Sampson cleared his throat. "Within a couple of solar days is the plan. I'd like to depart with Jace as soon as I can. In fact, the crew is prepping now."

He didn't bother mentioning the mess with Kascade or Humans First beyond the facts that the original kidnapper was assumed dead on a powerless ship. A ship now in the possession of another moon compound.

Sampson planned to pass on information about the terrorist group in person. Being in the tech haven of the universe where anyone could listen in and the nature of what he'd seen on those holo-screens made him aware that such conversations were better without electronic communications involved.

Al stroked his beard a couple times then sighed. "Then you'll let us know once you depart, and we'll set a meeting location. We are still a solar day out from the asteroid belt. Caught a bad stream."

The rings under the Al's eyes and the way he gathered his wife close to him scratched at Sampson's caged heart. Al wanted to see his kid, wanted to keep his family safe.

"Give me a minute. Gina, transfer this call to Dottie so the Smiths can see their son."

Both Al and Loyda perked up straightaway.

"Thank you, Sampson," Loyda offered right before the connection disappeared.

Only then did he slump against the chair. This mess — seeing parents so eager for a simple glance at their child — exhausted him. In some ways he could empathize with the longing, similar to how he longed for Zasha. But, at the same time, he was envious of how one individual could be wanted so much.

Except, he had no time to dwell. Not with all the additional messages he had to send — Sweet on Eden, and another to Emilio and Toni, who were wrapping up their gig and eager to be back on *Gina*.

Another problem Sampson would need to solve because the flash he needed from the Smiths remained a few days away, then he could buy Gina. This mess with Humans First proved he needed to get toward his goals of exploration a little faster and move past this small corner of the universe filled with suffering.

Right after he sent the last message, tired of speaking, was when Zasha stomped onto the command deck.

"Why are we prepping to leave? Doc and Lee said you want to be on your way back towards Jupiter in the next six solar hours."

"Yep." He nodded and yawned. "After we all get a couple hours' shut-eye. Care to join me?"

She frowned and crossed her arms. "You can't be serious."

He had to hope she'd back down because it was either sleep or have a conversation he feared more than anything. "As serious as a person who has gone nearly an entire day without rest. I would think you need a little as well. We all do. Sleep isn't something you should play around with. I've read enough texts —"

"Enough!" Zasha stomped her foot hard against the floor.

"What's the problem, Zasha?"

"You damn well know."

Sampson could think of five possibilities straightaway, including the ones where he had the right to be angry more than she did. He yawned again. "I'm not a mind reader. Just speak."

"We're leaving and there's still so much to be done. They need someone to take charge, to protect them. You could fill those shoes."

He laughed, and some of his fear melted away. "You're not the one who is being serious now. We should go to bed. Talk about this after a nap. Or two."

Standing, he reached for her, but she pulled back. "No. You could take charge. Be the leader these people desperately need. Someone who is smart and can see how problems can be fixed."

"And who has no desire whatsoever in being tied to a single place. My home is in the sky, here on this ship with Gina."

"Someone needs to step up." Zasha spread her arms wide. "You are the perfect choice. A good leader isn't someone who wants the power."

This whole conversation sat in the realm of unexpected. He planned for her to be upset because they would take away her leverage...her way back into Kascade's favor, or her transportation back to her leader, but not this half-spaced idea of him leading a moon compound.

He'd misjudged her again, though. This appreciation for his capabilities and belief in him surpassed his wildest dreams. Sure, he received random praise from the other crew members from time to time, but nothing like this. A bit of pressure hit him behind the eyes and numbness slinked through him. *She asks for the impossible.*

"I don't see how I am the only logical choice. These people had a leader and someone before them — probably a whole slew of folks who lead them successfully. They don't need me in the least. If I don't volunteer, there will be another."

Zasha growled in frustration, and he reached for her again. This time she grabbed him back, gripping his arms tight like a vise. "This could be a future for you. A place to belong."

"It's not my job." And Gina needed him. This ship, the AI, the stars…they needed him. A bunch of people who would pretend to care for him until something better came along — those who would only want him if he had something to offer…giving away pieces of himself until nothing remained. Until he betrayed everything he believed in. *Kascade did that.*

She pulled him close and hugged him. "Sampson, it could be. You can be more than whatever it is you're trying for. I know you love this ship, love the person you are when you're here, but freedom among the stars is unrealistic outside of the uppers and lowers because these ships are powered by dead people. You want to be admired for that big brain of yours? Then step up and use it."

Sampson didn't know what to say besides what he'd already stated — that he wasn't interested in taking over. Leaving Gina wasn't an option for him, and Zasha refused to listen to his answers, no matter how many times he restated them, so he did the only thing left.

He kissed her.

She didn't fight the touch of their lips, not at all. Instead, she melted against him. Within seconds, they were as hot and heavy as days past.

Too bad they weren't already in her quarters. No way could they take things further here on the command deck.

He finally broke away from her, his heartbeat pounding. "Let's head to bed. We can talk about it later. We both need rest."

The hazy, lust-filled look in her eyes melted away, anger renewing in those golden depths. "No, we aren't done. Did you think you could kiss me and fuck me into submission?"

He shook his head even as she stepped back, away from their embrace, once more leaving him cold. "No, I don't. This day has been a lot. I'm only stating we can rest, then talk about this when our heads are both fresh and our concentration's in full focus."

"My concentration is fine. My mind's never been clearer. I tell you these people need help, sharing this with the one person I've always believed helps others, and instead you turn away from the opportunity."

She kept pushing, and the truth sat at the bottom of his throat, aching to emerge. To confess his heart, which would hurt and wound. So, he clamped his mouth shut.

Him not saying anything didn't stop her though. "Tell me something. Give me a reason to accept this sudden disinterest in the wellbeing of innocent people. This horrible lack of caring for those who have less than you."

He could only take so much. Gina's light blinked blue as if she meant to interfere, but he held his hand up. *No, this is battle I can fight.*

"No one has ever cared for me, except the people on this ship, and only because I'm useful and it's convenient. There's only one person who's ever bothered to show me I'm worth their time, worth anything, as just me. So no, I'm not fast to jump on an opportunity where I won't be thanked for my sacrifice or where I'll be ditched when the next Kascade shows up with an ill-thought-out, brilliant-sounding idea.

"I want more than a simple what I can do for someone else. I want to have something for me for once. To surround myself with what I want and people who can appreciate more than what my big brain can do for them."

Zasha stumbled backward a few steps as if he'd slapped her.

The words he'd let explode into existence weren't all correct. He'd forgotten to mention her, how *she* was the person he talked about, but none of it really mattered. She'd become like the rest—she wanted him to do useful things.

Then she growled, her body elevated slightly as if her rage dawned like a near-burnt out star, assumed dead but only asleep till woken. "Then you're a fool, because doing things for people won't earn you love or blind admiration. Selfless action, sharing your abilities with others around you, enriches your life."

* * * *

Zasha hurt all over, exhaustion creeping into her limbs, despite the lies she'd told stating otherwise. At first Sampson's offer to sleep, to rest in his arms in a bed, tempted her along with his needy kiss. Yet, the truth and fear remained. If she took him up on his offer, by the time she woke up they would no longer be at the moon compound.

She didn't trust Sampson to take off without a second consideration for what still needed to be done.

Her temper and frustration remained clouded too. Knowing what the compounds did with bodies and seeing the processing performed by a couple of moonies, who'd said they were trained in the art, didn't renew her trust in whatever Kascade's plan involved.

No, she started to think the information that Gina had shared with her only a solar hour before might have been right. She'd sought out Sampson in the moon base ops room, only to find he'd already returned to the ship.

Instead, she'd been met by Gina's voice and the recall and playback of dozens of videos, communications and other horrifying things, solidifying her growing doubt and confirming the very reason she'd been allowed to join Humans First.

"We're all cogs in the system," Jennifer had once said.

Zasha had repeated the mantra every time a guild member had turned up dead at the hands of APU or when they'd had to ditch a compromised safe house. As usual, Zasha had been presented with the same shit, only a different fatching day.

The question still remained, who would take charge of this base? Kascade and those in Humans First had led the running and maintenance for this compound. Without those leaders, the group that remained wouldn't make it. At least not at first — they would have to trade and barter everything they had. That was the way these compounds operated, according to Gina.

The future had been laid out for Zasha, along with the past, and she'd been living in some ignorant utopian fairytale, falsely following Kascade's mantras of positivity and light when there were none. The same fake reality where the APU was responsible for the suffering here, and not the system the uppers had created. A false belief that the moonies latched on to, all too eager to believe they were victims instead of the ones holding the power.

Kascade wanted to end the system, according to what Gina discovered, but how she still wasn't sure. So, when Zasha had gone to find Sampson, she'd been hoping he'd agree to stay, at least for a little while.

Then they could figure out a solution together. To help these people rise above a system meant to keep them dependent on the uppers for technology in exchange for the basic necessities they should already have, like antibiotics. Thank goodness for Gina and for Doc's stores.

All the marijuana in the compound and their tech wouldn't provide them with enough supplies to fight their injuries.

Except, Sampson had fallen back on old wounds and deep-seated fears, running scared. She let out a small sob, trying to physically expel her disappointment.

Sampson frowned. "That's not what I meant."

"This is bullshit. The biggest amount of crap I've heard in years. You're still running, worried you'll never be loved, when these people are hurting, and injured. You want to punish someone, I'm right here. If you're still so upset and afraid you won't get what's owed to you, it's too late. I love you."

He shook his head.

"You don't believe me?"

Sampson sighed. "We can't... Love won't stop someone from leaving. Love doesn't always mean acceptance or trust or loyalty."

"Really? You're grasping at straws, anything to hold on to whatever misguided determination you have."

"Not true." He crossed his arms, closed himself off.

"Then maybe we should ask Gina. I'm sure she could tell us the answer from a logical perspective."

"Leave her out of this." The fear in those green eyes was like that of a starved, wild animal searching for an escape, but knowing damn well he was caught.

"No, you don't want your precious AI to tell you how you're wrong." Zasha had more to say, but instead she paced. Paced back and forth while Sampson continued to stand there, watching her warily, looking smaller and smaller as the minutes passed.

Finally, she stopped and recited what she'd learned from Gina. "These people don't have enough medical supplies or food stores to last more than another two weeks with as many injured. Trade routes, deliveries for tech and other obligations have to be met. The people appointed to maintain those relationships were leaders of Humans First and those people are gone or dead. In addition, they need to conduct a full catalog of the technology they have access to. These people need help and the only way to secure assistance is to know the full amount of what they possess. So far they have been given limited access by Kascade."

Sampson's eyebrows rose in suspicion. "Gina told you all this?"

"Yes, in the ops room. I was looking for you, but you'd already left. Gina has all the Humans First files, but there's some stuff she hasn't learned, amazingly. She needs your help. If you'll give her access to some older codebreaking tactics, she can hack the moon compound computers, completely. Give back control to the moonies who live here, at the very least."

"No." Sampson shook his head. "I let her in to review records, but the possible safeguards...what if the compounds are hooked together? The risk's too great. Besides, this is a selfish run on her part. The moonies can appoint their own leaders."

"Any risk isn't yours to take."

The fury that rose in Sampson's green eyes was all too reminiscent of the past, but as much as she hated seeing a mirror image of herself cast backward, she needed him to know he wasn't truly in control anymore. He refused to help, to bother with this, so she'd charge forward without him.

His ship had surpassed her function and could operate without his help. Gina had even suggested Zasha give her access to the code-breaking information.

Zasha could do it, though she would take a little longer. Sampson had mentioned Gina being selfish and Zasha had sensed an alternative purpose. Whether the efforts were altruistic on Gina's part or not, Zasha wanted to unlock this information for the moonies.

Sampson began to pace, as he ran his fingers through his hair and tugged on the ends. "What do you mean? If something happens to Gina, it affects everyone on this ship. Everyone. If she gets stranded or goes out of order, who's going to fix her? Me, and we'll all be stuck here. Which would work out well for you, of course."

"Yes, except I want this to provide help. To leave the Moonies more equipped than before." *And learn the whole truth.*

"Never happen."

Zasha sighed. "Like I said before, this isn't your choice. Not in the least bit and if you won't help, I'll do it."

"Gina?" Sampson sounded lost, confused, and a bit sad.

"Yes, Captain."

"Tell me. You weren't the one to suggest this?"

Gina's light blinked twice, the hesitation there. "I did. I need into those files too. I can't tell you why yet, but it's important. The truth needs to be known."

Truths, hidden agendas…time to blow this bullshit wide.

"Fine, but I'm not doing it." Sampson hung his head and headed for the door.

Zasha reached for him, but he shrugged away and turned on her.

"No, you don't get to pretend this is okay or act like the two of you didn't align against me. You both plotted this little thing before you walked in here, Zasha. This was never about me leading or stepping up. You were manipulating my emotions, hoping to appeal to some false idea about me that you clung to. Throwing love at me like it would change my mind. I won't be a pawn, and you should have come to me with the blunt truth. I'm going to bed, but when I wake up, we take off whether you two are done or not."

He headed out. Zasha wanted to say her chest didn't hurt, deny the ache taking residence. The same ache she'd carried for the first year after betraying him. She'd coated things a bit, hid all her plans and reasoning, but she loved him regardless. Her words were spoken from a place of truth, not lies. The history between them still engulfed the present no matter what.

"Zasha, I'm ready to begin working to access the code skills when you are ready."

Looking around, Zasha walked over to Dottie's chair and took a seat. "Walk me through the file location, and I'll do my best."

Time to break into somewhere else she didn't belong.

Chapter Fourteen

Two hours was what it took to crack into Gina's computer matrix and enhance her skills, per Gina's request. Opening the floodgates to knowledge wasn't so hard. What came next was more impressive than Zasha could imagine.

Hundreds of terabytes of data were unlocked and analyzed. Zasha tried to keep up with the bits and pieces flashing across the holo-screens, but her weary body gave up and she fell asleep at some point.

When she woke, startled by a beeping noise on the panel, Gina's voice rang out clear.

"I have unearthed all the answers. Everything the communications pointed to, right in front of everyone's eyes, but still invisible. We needed the last bits to connect the dots."

Zasha rubbed at her eyes and sat up straight. "What time is it?"

"We've got about one solar hour before Sampson wants to depart."

The impending threat of departure got her blood pumping, because she needed to look over all of this before then and get a plan together…and hopefully, keep Sampson from leaving.

They had some personal things to resolve, but Zasha still had the will to fight, for them and for the future.

"Show me."

Gina started to manipulate the holo-screens and going through the information, piecing everything together.

"Kascade is building an army of ships, working with Mars and using tech the APU doesn't have access to. It's big tech, the kind where AIs are powering synths and piloting ships."

"Synths?"

Gina's light blossomed in bright blue, the topic obviously one of excitement for her. "Synthetic humans. The concept is something Sampson mentioned once. The idea is referenced in many books and stories. Androids, they were sometimes called. Regardless of the name, the process is where an AI gets a body, no longer limited to interactions through a computer or sound system, but fully functioning."

Zasha's mouth dropped. This would be huge—with AI pilots for ships, there wouldn't be a need for humans to maintain anything and if pilots were successful, how long before they crafted armies? "Are they building these synths for the ships?"

"I can see where they have created a limited number of them. Not enough to use as a military force. The attack on Darren's stolen vessel was a trial run, after they tested some of the tech on the moonies themselves. Kascade attacked his own people."

Zasha clenched her fists and pounded them against the back of a nearby chair. *I'll kill him.* "Gina, can you tell me if Kascade has already made it to Mars?"

"Judging from surveillance, yes. He's there and plotting his next move. There is discussion of a potential show of force, but debate on where the display would occur."

Zasha stood up and stretched, the concept of an idea slowly formulating. "We have to wake Sampson and the others. Also, alert those of the Humans First still in the compound. Everyone needs to know the truth."

"Then what?"

"Get them to command deck and, by then, I'll figure it out."

Gina's light flashed acknowledgment, and Zasha ran her hands through her hair, loose from her restless sleep. She needed to convince them, show them. But even the most convincing argument could fail in the face of desperation, blind faith or complacency.

* * * *

Nearly a solar hour later, Sampson sauntered through the command deck doors, looking every bit as grouchy and grumbly as he had when he departed the night before. And still as handsome as hell. She wanted to wrap her arms around him and apologize for the argument they'd had. Tell him she'd do whatever he wanted. This was what love made a person do, act dumb.

She'd settle for showing him the insanity and proving why leaving now would be a horrible idea.

He was the last to show up for her meeting, but Zasha had expected as much. Of course, the ship wasn't en route to Jupiter as he'd intended and that probably contributed to his mood.

Dottie and Doc hovered near Lee, who had Jace strapped to her. A strange sight, Lee with a kid. The kid in question gnawed on apple slices, one in each hand. Jace definitely had the better end of the deal.

The Humans First members present were a couple, Rosh and Terry. Zasha hated seeing Terry so torn up, but the woman had appeared determined to show up with her husband.

She'd be the challenger, if her steadfast loyalty to Kascade held.

Sampson of course broke the silence. "Gina said this was urgent and it's delaying our departure, so can we get moving?"

Zasha sighed, breathing out slowly releasing the urge to give an equally petulant retort. Sampson could infuriate her with his impatience. In this way he still acted like a boy, eager to follow his path, a lot like a certain ship captain who owned Gina and damn anyone else who got in the way.

"Agreed. What is this about? We still have injured to care for and problems to solve." Terry chimed in.

"This is a bigger one." Gina's blue light rippled along the wall. She'd told Zasha that she'd decided to quit hiding.

Sampson's scowl got deeper.

Rosh looked startled and gripped his wife's hand. "What was that?"

"The ship...it's powered by AI," Zasha replied, holding out her hands as if it would keep the room calm. "But this meeting is not about Gina. It's about Kascade building an army of ships in his partnership with Mars. They're using whatever technology they've developed here to outfit them as well. Gina and I believe that he plans to attack the APU."

Silence reigned for about twenty seconds and the room erupted.

"No way," Terry said with a small gasp.

"Any attack would provoke an all-out war," Doc chimed in.

"Impossible." Sampson elbowed his way through his crew and Rosh and Terry. "He wouldn't dare."

Zasha frowned. "Gina, show them."

The holo-screen illuminated, and the evidence was displayed all over again. Gina showcased the bits of communications, the approved work orders, transfers of flash and powder, the contracts with the mercenaries. By the time she'd finished, the room was so silent that Jace's slurps and chomps on the apple slices were the only sounds to echo along the walls.

Finally, one voice spoke first. Sampson's. "It's not our problem."

Zasha took a step back, her chest aching. "You're wrong. It is, and I for one want to fight this. There's time for us to go to Mars, to take a stand and do reconnaissance while we send a message to the APU."

"Why do we care about a war? The APU won't go quietly, and they deserve it." This from Terry, who still gripped Rosh's arm but possessed a look questioning the proof in front of her.

"The APU didn't attack the base. Kascade did."

Rosh angled around Sampson and put a finger in Zasha's face. "You are an outsider, someone who rode in looking for a safe haven, convenient for a spy and APU sympathizer. You were here to infiltrate us from within."

"You need to put your finger down or I'll do it for you." Zasha's patience thinned considerably. When evidence was put in front of someone as plain as day and they still clung to false ideas or came up with new conspiracies to fight the truth, she couldn't be passive.

Rosh screwed his face up like a shriveled piece of dried fruit. "I don't need to do anything—"

Zasha reached out and snapped his finger. In half.

The moan was coupled with a scream, as Rosh crumpled to the floor. "You broke my finger!"

"I told you to get it out of my face."

Lee laughed. Zasha eyeballed her and the kid, who'd gotten to enjoy the show.

"Shit," the assassin mumbled, as she turned away from the scene, shielding Jace's eyes.

Sampson stepped between Zasha and Rosh. "Violence solves nothing."

"Tell that to them." Zasha nodded at Rosh and Terry. "Seems they think it's the only thing we can do to solve our problems. We need to stop Kascade. Before his madness puts the galaxy into a civil war. No one can afford fighting everywhere. Not the people on the moon or on Earth."

"They could if they chose to," cried out Terry.

"Why would you choose war?" The question from Zasha's lips hit the air with such disgust. Wars never won anything, except more loss.

"When everything is taken from you and what little you've been left isn't enough. Talking only works so much. Maybe we leave Kascade to his own devices." Sampson was siding with them.

Unbelievable.

Zash growled and fisted her hands. "Well, Gina disagrees with me, and now I'm asking this crew if they'll stand with me on taking Gina to Mars and stopping this disaster."

"That's not something you call out in the middle of a room. Especially since you haven't discussed this with the ship's captain." Sampson hated how his voice sounded. Small, almost whimpering, like a kernel of fear was growing within him.

He'd barely slept, tossing and turning, physically wrestling with Zasha's words, Gina's betrayal and wondering if what he wanted mattered. Where did all this fit in, and would he be better leaving everything behind?

Only to wake to more chaos and now she'd cut him off at the knees, cut away his command. This had been his mission, his job in the beginning and slowly, but surely, Zasha had sneaked in and infiltrated everything. Rooted everyone away from him, including Gina. Regardless of what Zasha said, she'd effectively operated in opposition of him with every step. When he'd said left, she'd chosen right. Maybe this had been the truth of them from the get-go. She had her causes and no amount of love or appreciation stopped her.

He needed to fight back, but fists weren't the option here. He wouldn't win in hand-to-hand combat against her anyway. "Can everyone leave the room, please?"

Lee walked out first. "Sounds like a great plan. I'll be back after I give this little guy a bathroom break."

Dottie and Doc followed, with Doc stopping beside Rosh and encouraging the married couple to follow him to the medbay.

"What are you doing? We need to make a choice, now. Not later. Time is already running out." Zasha huffed.

Once they'd all cleared out, he pressed a button on the wall panel and closed the command deck doors. "I need to speak with you separately. Not with a room full of people listening."

She threw her hands in the air. "What then? You're sad, upset at me for showing the truth, weren't you saying this crap from the moment I saw you in the bar. How we can't trust Humans First?"

"I said it, but..." Sampson approached Zasha slowly. He wanted, stupidly to get close to her as if the physical connection between them could somehow stop them tearing each other down with words and abrupt action.

She stopped moving as he approached. "You're not talking."

"Come here." Sampson reached for her and at first her gaze darted around like a cornered animal, ready to dodge and run. At the last second, some sort of recognition dawned in her eyes and she let him touch her.

He wrapped himself around her, pulled her in close. "I get all this makes you angry."

"Sampson, I'm furious. You ran off to the ops room. You didn't stand there hearing the cries of those women, the children...innocent blood all over the landing bay and it could have been prevented. Then Gina showed you everything, and you won't join the fight."

Sampson tensed, with her in his arms. He didn't want to, but the accusation elevated things anew. She tried to pull back, and he let her go.

"What now?" She threw her hands in the air. "It's true. You're running from any possibility of getting involved, selfishly avoiding the very opportunity to gain more fawning and appreciation. As needy as you are, I'm shocked."

Her anger cleansed him of any amorous inkling and desire to use their personal connection to spare them from another blow-up.

"Needy?"

"Desperate for validation. You keep acting like everyone wants you for a single purpose, but the truth is we often can't see beyond what's happening each day. We take what we can from those moments and try to show appreciation in a universe not guaranteed to give us anything back. All you can do is leave the biggest mark possible on the world right now. Quit thinking the people closest to you will leave at the first attempt you take to do what's right."

Sampson clenched his fists as Zasha's words washed over him. She'd become some vengeful angel and, in the process, appeared determined to destroy everything in her path to her end game.

"Appreciate the self-analysis, but why don't you look at your own damn self too?"

"Oh, I am." She leaned against the holo-table and stared him down. "I take a good look every solar day."

He stepped forward, crowding her space. "Really? So, you're fully aware you're doing everything you can to chase redemption for all the blood you spilled. Willing to push everyone aside at some desperate mission to earn a good name for yourself. Sometimes you have to live with your actions. Suck it up and move forward."

Tears were forming in the corners of her eyes and Sampson hated it, naturally he started to tear up as well. This hurt. All of it.

"Kascade's battle isn't our fight."

She lifted her arms, fists ready to pound against his chest, and he grabbed her forearms with both hands as they crashed toward him. "Don't say that."

"We don't have to do this. I turn over the kid and we go, we run. Quit fighting battles trying to atone for past sins and live for yourself."

She crumpled against him, letting him hold her once more as her tears turned into a small waterfall and she sobbed openly. He understood, and he cried with her.

"I can't, Sampson."

"Not even for us?"

"You say we could run, but the notion is foolish. You want to be treated like an adult but dream like a child."

Sampson reeled back, stepping away from her as if she had wailed on him in a physical attack.

"What? I'm speaking truth."

"Go fatch yourself." He turned on his heel and headed for the door. "I'm finishing the original job. I don't care what you say."

Once outside the command deck, he headed toward the galley. "Gina, where's Lee?"

Blue surrounded him, a halo of bright light. "Sampson, Zasha is right. We need to stop this."

"You too? Somehow, I don't believe you're in this because of the survival of humankind, Gina. Besides, why fight for people who would love to open you up and exploit your capabilities?"

He made it to the galley and nothing. Not a single person there.

Medbay then.

Turning around he stalked towards the medbay, picking up his pace in the presence of Gina's lack of verbal response.

Only her blue light chased after him as he stalked away, but a minute or so later she spoke. "I care. Though there are other things I seek to learn."

Sampson scoffed. "I figured. Everyone has their own angle. Is this worth possibly dying over? You fly into a potential war zone, you won't be an ally to either side. They could blow you up."

The medbay was mysteriously empty as well.

"Gina, seriously where the hell is everyone?"

He stood in the corridor like someone lost in their own nightmare, with nothing but a lonely future staring him down. "You ditch me, and Emilio and Toni will blame me for losing you."

"Then come with us."

"Quit stalling. Where are they?"

Gina's blue light blinked to yellow. For an AI, she somehow understood guilt, and at least provided a facsimile. "Zasha asked me to invite Doc, Dottie and Lee back to the command deck."

"I should have passed them on their way there." Sampson ran a hand through his hair and tugged on the ends gently. This entire fatching day could melt away. He longed to be back asleep, or in bed with Zasha in his arms.

"No, Lee was in her quarters with Jace, and Doc and Dottie were seeing the Humans First couple off the ship. It's okay, your timing was off. You're welcome to come to the talk too."

Sampson sighed, slumping against the nearest wall and sinking to the floor. "Right. So, you can all tell me how wrong I am. No, I need you to send another message, reach out to the moonies. I need a ship."

He could hear her unspoken response. This crew was known to be way too self-sacrificing, especially when innocents were involved. How many times had Emilio and Toni agreed to come to the aid of people who didn't deserve help? Too many.

Except, an innocent kid could help inspire the action of the APU. Sampson didn't miss the possibility, but for once he didn't want to be waging wars against foes. He wanted to be at peace with the people he loved.

It seemed no matter where he went, the universe tried to fatch with him.

A few minutes later Gina's blue light came back. "The moonies state they have a shuttle they will allow you to use, free of charge. Since you helped with everything."

"Good." Sampson pushed himself up on his knees then stood. His heart ached, heavy with failure. Though he still needed to officially be present at the mutiny.

"I'm going to head to the command deck now."

"I expected no less, Captain."

Chapter Fifteen

Zasha angrily swiped away her tears and straightened herself up as Lee walked in first with Jace strapped to her, followed by Doc and Dottie.

"Good, looks like everyone got my message. The same question is still on the table. Gina and I want to head to Mars, but we can't do it alone."

Dottie rolled her eyes and hugged Doc's arm a little tighter, her dark skin a contrast to his lighter pigment. "You mean, you want us to run the suicide mission with you. Gina, bless you, but there is no way you know what we're headed for."

Gina's light blinked. "You are correct. I don't have all the information, but enough to make some extrapolations. I believe we can infiltrate Mars and potentially shut down the ship building operations with little issue."

"Who's doing this shutting-down piece?" Lee asked.

Zasha pointed at the assassin then at herself. "We are. The two of us, a sneak in-and-out-style ops. With our combined skills, it shouldn't be a problem. It will take at least a solar day to get to Mars, and we can finalize any planning from there."

Jace spoke up then. "Apple."

The kid had a never-ending appetite.

"And what about him?" Doc asked, holding out his hand for Jace to grab hold of and shake up and down.

"I'm taking him to Jupiter." Sampson's voice boomed across the command deck from the entrance. He marched into the room, and Zasha froze in place, shocked he'd even come back and fearful he might try to derail everything all over again.

Splitting up would be chaos — no way Zasha could agree. "That's — "

"Nope, not arguing. Everyone here, Gina included, can get involved in a foolhardy plan, but putting the kid in danger isn't an option. Not one we can sign up for and hope to survive."

She frowned, frustrated by the words he was saying and how logical they sounded. She wanted to disagree, to keep him with her because to be honest she didn't know when he left if they'd see each other again.

Too bad she'd let her emotions run wild, instead of taking herself for a nap. Too bad how in less than twelve solar hours they were going to be faced with splitting apart and maybe another argument.

Too stubborn. Those were the words Jennifer had used to describe Zasha. So stubborn she'd cut her nose off to spite her face.

"You're not wrong. It's a good idea. Keep the kid safe, get him back to his parents, but Lee could do that. Even Doc and Dottie." *Lies.* Because she needed an assassin like Lee, a pilot to maneuver if something happened to Gina and a medic like Doc if they got hurt.

Sampson glanced over at the others and shook his head. "Nope, it's got to be me. The person who takes the job finishes the job. Emilio and Toni have always run things the same way, and I'm not going to change or stop now. I'll finish the job and see everyone back on Eden."

There were words left unspoken there, things not being said. Zasha sensed frustration rolling off Sampson in subtle waves, almost as if he were afraid to come too close.

"Then my question remains for the rest of you. Are you in? Come with Gina and I to Mars or go with Sampson to finish the original job."

Lee was the first to clear her throat. "Normally, I would stick to the original job no matter what, but this thing with Humans First...a Mars-built ship armada. I mean, that's important too. Can't say I can count on the APU to come busting in until it's too late. So, I'm sticking with Gina."

Dottie nodded in agreement and squeezed Doc's hand.

"I go where Dottie goes, so I guess that's Mars for now." Doc squeezed back and the pair leaned on each other.

"All right." Sampson clapped his hands together and walked over towards the door. "Then Doc, Lee, can you ready the kid and pack together enough stuff for him to make it a max of three solar days? I'm going to pack a bag. The moonies said they could get me a ship. It's not big, but I'll make it."

Zasha opened her mouth, but Sampson had already made it out of the door before she could voice an objection. Her heart beat oddly, like a ship with a malfunctioning engine.

"I'd imagine you have about an hour, maybe less before he plans to get out of here." Dottie had stepped over beside her. "One thing I would never do is let someone I love leave without speaking my mind."

Love? A pesky word, but it still existed, it was what she'd felt for Sampson the moment he'd rescued her from a damn burning vessel. *Even when we kept hurting each other.*

"Why bother? He couldn't wait to get away from me. We already said all we wanted to."

Dottie clutched Zasha's shoulder and gave it a light squeeze. "He's angry. Doesn't see eye-to-eye with what you're doing, but he loves you."

Zasha scoffed, her eyes fluttering closed as she did. When she opened them, a silver knife flashed in front of them.

Lee stood toe to toe with her. "Don't dismiss it, because he fatching loves you. You're not worth it— boy is too damn good for you. Regardless, Dottie's right. You can't leave without talking to him. Don't let these disagreements between you end things."

Zasha crossed her arms a little tighter than normal. "I can't—"

"Just go to him." Dottie nudged her in the direction of the door. "Don't let your last words be from anger."

So Zasha went, blindly, not really focused on the destination. "Gina, where is Sampson?"

"His quarters." Blue lights blinked around her and followed in her wake.

"Will you open the door for me?" Because the fear of him not answering lodged deep inside her, making it impossible to raise her hand.

"Yes."

She smiled. "I'm surprised you agreed."

The blue light blinked twice. "At this point I'm like everyone else, choosing something else over him. What does it matter if I make him angry again, as long as you two get a chance to resolve your previous disagreements?"

Zasha's pace increased to a light jog down the hallway, reflecting her eagerness to get to him. But what would she say?

Because the words coming to her now didn't make sense. This thing between them had proved difficult to navigate in regular circumstances, but then their goals never seemed to align. He'd been hurt by her and the others, even by the ship he called a best friend.

Fresh dread kindled up like a small fire in a trolling motor. She couldn't smother it like a little water would do. No, this built higher and higher until she stood before Sampson's door, the worry and fear of recrimination threatening to send her running in the other direction.

His door opened at Gina's command.

Sampson stood, his back to her, shoving random clothes into a green duffel. "Lee, I don't want to talk. Meet me in the landing bay with Jace and his stuff."

She hesitated. Gina's light blinked green.

Damn.

A deep breath then she took the first step over the threshold.

Sampson turned to see who'd come in. "Zasha?" Confusion marred his features before morphing into sadness. It seeped into his eyes, his slouched frame, and he dropped the bag.

"Gina let me in," she said.

He gave a small shake of his head and reached down for the bag. "She would. What do you want? Because honestly, you've already done your worst. I'm trying to keep it together, to depart and do what I need to with what little dignity I have left and I can't…"

As he trailed off, she marched over to him, circled up underneath his half-open arms and looped her own over his neck. "I needed you to know one thing. I love you."

Then she kissed him.

* * * *

Her showing up in his quarters he hadn't expected. Her kissing him, one more time, was a fantasy turned true.

Her confession of love re-stated, and not in anger, buoyed him after all the words they'd exchanged in their last two encounters on the command deck. Things hadn't gone well and the truth about their plans and futures never aligning hurt more than when she'd left the first time. So the words were bittersweet.

Yet, their joined lips turned into tongues and more. He couldn't keep his hands still, as he heard the door hiss shut, effectively locking them inside together.

They were completely alone and for this one moment he'd take every second they had until someone banged down the door. It didn't take long for the clothes to come off or for them to reach his bed and tangle up there.

She broke their touch and kissing first. "I want to suck you off."

"And I want my mouth on your pussy," he replied.

Her answering smile and shove against his chest told him for once they agreed. She repeated the actions they'd shared in her quarters before. Him flat on his back, with her thighs straddling his head, her wet center pressed against his waiting mouth.

She tasted lightly sweet and salty, a heady mixture equal parts tantalizing and familiar. He enjoyed it. As much as some people shied from the act, he liked teasing her into a frenzy with his tongue and teeth, listening to her gasps and taking note of how her body reacted to his efforts.

Sure, the efforts to concentrate on pleasing her were constantly warring against her own ministrations on his cock. He enjoyed the amount of work it took to stay focused, as if they were both still playing a game in who could make the other come first.

This is what I'll miss. As she crested over, her legs locking around him, her crying out his name, tears began to flow. He stifled the small whimper as he licked up the rest of her juices.

She immediately released his cock and flipped her body around, her face aligned with his once more. "Sampson?"

He shook his head. The words were weak, made him weak. He loved her, and she was leaving him with a one-time parting gift. She kissed his tears then licked them away. Putting her lips to his, she tongued him the same way he'd fucked her.

"I love tasting myself on you. It's okay. I know how this feels."

The sadness immediately dulled replaced by anger, frustration at her. This woman who said she loved him could barge in all over again then walk away. *Never.*

He gripped her and flipped her over onto her back with a growl. "Never again."

Zasha, eyes wide, gripped him back, her nails biting into his upper arms. "What?"

"Being with anyone else won't be like this. Won't mean what this does." He impaled her in a single stroke, sinking deep, letting her feel every inch.

She gasped.

He pulled out, then returned. Back and forth, a rough push and pull with the slow pace rapidly increasing.

Soon she was holding on to him as he fucked her with all the force he could muster. As if the harder he drove into her, the more he could imprint a memory of him. He wanted her to be unable to even consider another man in her bed, knowing they wouldn't fuck her like this.

He leaned down and whispered into her ear, "They won't eat your pussy until you scream. They'll never fuck you until your breath stutters from your body."

She moaned. "I'm going to—"

"You'll scream my name. I want to hear it echo off the walls." He'd become a demon possessed at this point, chasing the most incredible orgasm he could possibly have, his cock rock-hard.

Like a piston of steel ramming hard enough to power a slip drive. Seconds later he came, and she did as well. She screamed his name so loud he could swear it vibrated through the room.

Sampson tried to gently roll off her but Zasha refused, lashing herself against his body and pulling him down against her. She took all his weight, what little he had, and held him.

The tears threatened again, but this time he felt moisture on his cheeks that wasn't from him. Lifting his head, he saw droplets of water seeping from her eyes and he gripped her tightly in return.

"I love you, too."

* * * *

Four solar hours later, Sampson took the bag Doc held out for him, then shook the older man's hand. Except the embrace didn't end there. No, the old man pulled him for a hug and squeezed the breath out of him.

"Be safe. Keep your engine primed and don't stop."

Sampson chuckled. "We'll be fine. It's you I'm worried about."

"Eh, Gina has us good and protected. See you on Eden." Doc ambled off.

Dottie replaced him, pulling a cap over Sampson's head. "I'm surprised Zasha isn't here to see you off?"

"She's resting."

Dottie winked at him. "I'm sure, but even so she should be here to say goodbye. Want me to have Gina message her?"

Sampson shook his head. No way in a black hole did he want to see her now. His resolve might falter, and he refused to cry in front of these people. The people he'd grown up with didn't need to see him acting like some little boy because he was separating himself from the woman he'd fallen for not once, but twice.

"She needs the rest, especially for whatever Gina has planned."

Dottie looked skeptical but gave him a hug and patted his cap-covered hair. "Be safe. Gonna miss your face, those smiles."

The older woman shook her head and walked over to Doc.

Then Lee approached.

"If you tell me to be safe —"

"Screw that. I'm going to tell you I packed a couple extra knives in the pack for Jace. He's strapped into the chair like Doc said he needs to be. There's a stasis pod in the back if you need it. Don't trust anyone."

Then she stopped talking, and they stared at each other for a minute. This woman had been like a surrogate sibling, almost a parent. They all had. From time to time, they had offered him advice, taught him things, but she'd always given him the most crap. This would be the first time he'd gone on a mission alone.

And— "I'm going to do something stupid." Lee pulled him in and hugged him tight.

Sampson froze underneath the assassin's sentimental moment, then hugged her back. A strange two seconds, for sure, filled with actions he never expected to be repeated again.

When she pulled away, he gave a small smile, and Lee punched him in the shoulder in return. "Get the job done, then get to Eden. Don't be late for the big party we're going to throw after we kick Kascade's ass."

Sampson rubbed his shoulder. "Sure, you got it."

Then he boarded the moonie ship and refused to look back. As promised, they'd gotten him a refurbished pleasure vessel with a reinforced hull and a slip drive. There was a small sleeping area off to the side of an even smaller galley. Any smaller and it would be a shuttle attached to *Gina's* hull.

Jace was already strapped into the spare seat on the bridge, a grin on his face when he saw Sampson. "We go Jupiter."

"Yep, kid. Taking you home to your parents. So be cool—it's going to be a long trip." Sampson belted himself in and walked through the pre-take-off procedures. It had been a long time since he'd had to do this himself. Gina took care of everything for him.

Everything. Shit, Gina.

He'd hadn't said goodbye to her or Zasha. He'd left Zasha to sleep and was still too frustrated at Gina for choosing this Mars mission over him. Since he'd saved her all those years ago, it was supposed to be her and him against the universe. Then she ditched at the first chance of more knowledge.

At the chance for a body.

Sampson knew Gina's innermost aspirations the same way he'd shared things with her. She dreamed of being human, of at least walking among humans, talking to them, eating with them, instead of being some omniscient observer only able to watch and never experience. Selfishly, Sampson never wanted a regular life for her, because to give her a body would mean she'd no longer need him or his support. She could function solely on her own.

"Jace, hungry." The kid pointed to himself and tried to squirm in his seat to point to the galley.

"You have to wait a bit, kid. At least let me get us into orbit."

"Okay." The small innocent reply wrapped itself around Sampson's heart, a tiny clamp of kindness latching on to him. Maybe Gina didn't need him, or at least she didn't think so, but for now this kid did.

The checklist, the launch—everything went smoothly and they were in the air and out of the moon's gravity in no time at all. Sampson transmitted his message to the Smiths as soon as they hit the currents and turned on the slip drive.

Normally, he'd ask Gina how long the trip would take, but now he had to read the holo-screen, calculate the travel time and try not to get misty-eyed about being on his own.

"Two days of travel, kid. Maybe less depending on the current. Your parents are meeting us at Callisto station."

"Hungry." Jace grinned at him and squirmed again, putting up his hand and pointing towards the back of the chair.

One-track mind. If *he* had been this hungry as a kid, no wonder his parents couldn't afford to feed him. Sampson put on the autopilot and unstrapped from the seat. He was tempted to leave Jace locked in position. A kid loose on a ship was a recipe for disaster. Instead, he'd let them both stretch their legs.

They headed to the galley and shared a quick meal. Right after Jace yawned. The only option for sleep was the stasis unit, because the bunks were tiny things that folded out from the wall, meaning the kid could roll off them.

"It's the unit for you. You fall and hit your head, your parents will take it out of my fee."

Jace nodded. "Mama, I want her."

"Soon, kid."

* * * *

Less than six solar hours later, Sampson rose from his bunk and headed to the pilot chair. Mars was in sight. The current he'd hopped on had moved a bit faster than expected, getting him farther out in near-record time. Being lighter than what Gina usually weighed had probably helped.

The kid, shockingly, still slept. Sampson saw no reason to wake him prematurely. They both needed all the rest they could get. Sampson checked all the readings and confirmed a message from the Smiths.

Continue updating with estimated time of arrival. We will be on Callisto station within hours.

Great. Yeah, the current moved fast, but not that fast. Then a proximity alarm went off.

Sampson looked down, and the holo-screen beeped. Shit, he'd give his right arm for Gina right now. She would have handled this.

He pressed the communications button. "This is the moon vessel, Moonlight." *How original.* "Please confirm why you are blocking my path?"

"Moon vessel, Moonlight, prepare to be boarded. This is the APU, and we will inspect your ship for contraband."

Fatch. The only problem with the moon vessels was they were used for shipments of supplies only and since the moonies traded with the APU, they had no weapons.

"Didn't see a need for them, my ass." The excuse Rosh and Terry had given when Sampson had queried about capabilities.

Sampson checked the pistol on his hip. His stunner, water torch and other gadgets were on his belt. The priority was the kid. He stumbled back to the stasis pod as the shuttle vibrated from the boarding tether locking on. He wasn't making it out of this one and forget making the rendezvous.

At least I have the kid safe for now.

"Let's hope they feel like taking us hostage."

Chapter Sixteen

A bright light had Sampson blinking his eyes. Only after he opened them did he recognize his surroundings enough that he tried to stand but couldn't. No, someone had strapped him to a chair with a length of rope, his feet to the legs, his mid-section and arms to the back.

"I see the Smith gang has gotten better at restraints," he offered up to the dark room outside of the light halo shining on him.

Something cold and wet splashed against his face. Sampson was damn thirsty but too afraid to stick his tongue out for a taste. The odor of the liquid was acidic, but it didn't burn his flesh.

"Shut up, boy. We'll do the talking around here," came from an older woman who stood off from the light, but her light blonde, near-white hair couldn't hide even in the dark.

Toni and Al's mom, and this was their family's bar. The Smiths themselves were a curious lot and

Alexander Smith would be pissed if his mother let something happen to his son.

"Where's the kid?"

"Safe. I won't let anyone harm him." Bebe Smith might have not been the best mother in the world, but she had a strange obsession with her kin. Though Toni still didn't speak to the woman and Sampson had no clue where Al fit into things.

Hell, what did it matter? He was going to be chained up to this chair for a while—he might even be left here—but no way would he become a member of a gang or cult. Nope, he'd done indentured service before and would die before he did it again.

Instead of dwelling on what he didn't know, the instincts and training Lee had passed down took over. He surveyed his surroundings the best he could.

He was definitely in the Watering Hole. The last time he'd been here, there'd been a big party celebrating Toni's homecoming. There were some memories of a shared kiss with a girl and of course the Smiths had sold out Toni to a drug lord, the one Emilio had been evading. They'd planned to tear up *Gina* and sell the crew. Thankfully, Emilio and Lee had saved them.

The first time Toni and the crew had gotten captured, the whole crew of lackeys had been there. This time, Sampson didn't get the celebrity treatment. No, only two men were in the room along with Bebe. One had a gun trained on him, and the other held the light.

Of course, any number of folks could be hiding in the back room or right outside, though Mars wasn't known for its fabulous views or anything. No, the red dust on the ground covered anything not underground or sealed up in a building. Terraforming had made it habitable, but not hospitable.

"Hey, I don't mean to rush anyone, but when are we gonna get to talking? I have plans."

"So do I." A new voice answered, one from behind him. The person Sampson couldn't see.

Sampson was tempted to try to twist his neck for a better view, but he couldn't imply interest. Lee always advised against showing the enemy any more than necessary.

"Really? Your plans can't be more important than mine."

The clink of boots, not gravs, but metal lined, tapped against the floor as the voice brought his face into the picture. A tall man, broad shouldered, long hair blond with a few streaks of silver, stood in front him. Random scars, the wrinkles of sun exposure and stone-cold gray eyes stared at Sampson, as if trying to sum up the total of his person.

Good luck, spacehole.

"Do you know who I am?"

Sampson shrugged. "A member of the Smith gang."

The truth was as plain as the haughty way the idiot carried himself and the tattoo on not one, but both wrists—the speaker was the leader who'd left his people to die at the hands of mercenaries. Kascade. But Sampson wanted to hear him say it.

"I'm Kascade. I lead the Humans First movement. We seek to stop the exploitation of humans being used for fuel by the APU to power their ships. Unfortunately, the APU doesn't really believe in doing what's best for humanity. They only think about themselves, which is why we have partnered with the Smith group and others here on Mars."

"You mean the gangs on Mars. Because Mars is a planet of gangs filled with people who happen to build ships and know how to race."

"Hey." Bebe stood from the stool she sat on and marched over to Kascade. Her hands on her hips, she sneered at him. "We are business folk, not gangs. A gang implies chaos and there's nothing chaotic about a little loyalty and order."

Sampson chuckled. "Oh sure, and what about Al, Bebe? He was trying to get everyone in the APU."

Bebe spat on the ground at Sampson's feet. "A shit deal, trying to ignite some peace agreement the APU will never adhere to. They can't enforce things from their glass houses. My son has been brainwashed by the damn parliament bitch wife he took. True love and a Mars rat's ass."

Kascade reached out and patted Bebe on the shoulder, turning her around as he did and guiding her back to her stool. "Calm yourself, Mrs. Smith. Have another drink. I'll talk to this one."

"This one, what the hell do you want? I need to get the kid and go. You can have your petty war, do whatever you want. I'm just trying to get paid for the job I did. The job you and your lackeys already messed up." The true story, if Kascade had tried to kidnap Jace a day later, would have been different.

Then I would have never seen Zasha.

Fatch, he couldn't regret what he'd experienced. Not at all. The time he'd had with her would be something he would hold on to for the rest of his life.

"They say you're an engineer, the best in the galaxy."

He shrugged. "People are easily impressed."

Bebe scoffed. "Don't give him no sass, boy, or I'll have Earl over here smack you a couple times."

Sampson growled. "I know my way around an engine."

"No, you fixed that fancy ship Toni flies on. Fixed it right up. You talked to my girl, Cassie. She said you couldn't stop babbling about how you removed the stoners' virus from her and fixed the AI, added extra security or some shit." Bebe laughed, then slammed her hand down on the bar. "Girl said she had to kiss you to get you to shut up. So high on yourself."

Heat rose in Sampson's cheeks. So, he'd bragged — he'd been trying to impress a girl and now even his poor attempt was being thrown back in his face. "Fatch you."

The guy with the light, who Sampson supposed was Earl, stepped forward, a hulking man of darkness, and punched him in the face.

Blood filled his mouth, a loose tooth possibly, and Sampson spit on the floor.

"You'll help me," Kascade said with a smile.

I'll die first. "I can't."

"Then you're a boy, not a man. Boys still hide from their truths, their talents, letting others dictate futures. You have a man's body but not those ideals."

Sampson did his best to keep his face passive, to push down the anger and let Kascade insult him. The words didn't hurt, not like the ones Zasha had already leveled at him. He'd become fully aware of his faults, but no matter what, he refused to give in to these idiots. He would never give up his life in the service of those meaning to harm masses of people.

Kascade crouched in front of him. "Last time, you will help me with my ships and my software issues."

Sampson drew on his hate then, all the frustration he held toward the people he loved and this idiot in front of him. Those who continued to make the universe more of a shit hole than it already was. He took those emotions, balled them up and trained them into the coldest stare he could muster.

"Like I said before, you can go fatch yourself, spacehole."

Kascade motioned with his fingers and the two lackeys moved in, the lamp switching off as they took turns beating on him.

Punches, slaps, kicks. By the time they finished, Sampson could barely take a breath without his entire ribcage screaming in agony. They picked the chair up, him along with it, and took him behind the bar, then stuffed him into a hole in the floor.

The landing hurt worse than the beating, his bruised and mangled body unable to do anything but absorb the impact with cold, packed Mars dirt. Small puffs of dust drifted upward, invading his nostrils, and the sneezes caused equal amounts of pain.

"Son of the devil!"

Kascade chuckled above him. "I've never been called that before, but here's what I'll do. I'm going to give you one more chance. Either help Humans First or you die."

With the offer made, what little light filtering down from the hole above his head disappeared with the shadow of Kascade leaning over the edge and leaving Sampson in darkness. He was still trapped in the chair, but the back pieces had loosened from the seat and gave him a little bit of ease.

He squirmed and winced at how much everything hurt. Getting out of the chair wouldn't get him closer to freedom.

"An answer, Sampson. Will you be a dead man or a live one?"

* * * *

Zasha sat in the galley, sipping a cup of coffee and swiping at her portable holo-screen. The plans were all there. "Gina, you're thorough."

"Yes, I try. Emergency transmission coming in, from the Smiths. Do you want me to connect you?"

She took a deep breath. She hadn't been prepared for talking with the Smiths, or anyone, for that matter. Dottie, Doc, Lee and Gina had all looked to her as some sort of captain or leader on this particular mission of mess. She'd never led anything. At least nothing with a quantity of people and usually those assignments had been limited to two other people, tops, ending lives, stealing things. In this case, they were trying to take over the ships using Gina's superior AI before Kascade launched them.

"Yeah, connect me." She sat up straight and tried to look not aloof.

The screen on the wall crackled as the connection finalized, Ambassador Al Smith's face appeared first, his red beard a dead giveaway. "Who are you?"

Zasha flattened her palms against the galley table and summoned strength. "I'm Zasha, the acting captain for *Gina* and you're Ambassador Smith."

"Where is Sampson and my son?" His green eyes narrowed, suspicion clouding his gaze. Sure, she got it, she was the unknown entity.

"Sampson left more than a solar day ago, headed for a rendezvous with you and your wife. As to where, he didn't tell us." Deep down, Zasha remained a little bitter over his abrupt absence.

She'd woken hours after his departure to a cold spot next to her in bed. No letter, no message left with Gina…he'd ditched, like the words they'd shared had never meant anything. The ache inside her chest had bloomed then and nothing she'd done since had removed it. Disappointment remained, because she had hoped those last words and moments implied Sampson would stay with her or at least come back.

Al frowned. "They never met us at our planned location. We have received a notice of a ransom from Kascade with Humans First, and I need to know if Sampson sold our son to the movement for more flash."

"What do you mean?"

Another face appeared on the screen, a woman who had to be Al's wife. "We mean, Zasha Gustaf, ex-mercenary and Humans First recruit, your leader has our son. We want to believe Sampson wouldn't give our boy away for flash, but honestly it's hard to trust anyone these days."

"He would never." Zasha clenched her fists in offense on Sampson's behalf. "Gina can confirm the ship he departed on as well as the fact he'd planned to meet up with you."

Al embraced his wife, hugging her close to him. The sight gave Zasha a momentary jealousy. "We would appreciate that."

"What will you do?" Zasha had to know because any change in plan could affect what her and Gina were working on.

Al sighed and Loyda shook her head, but the former comforted his wife. "We will have to pay the ransom. My child is worth more than anything the APU could threaten me with. I'll pay what he asks for. If anything happens to him, I can't guarantee that the APU won't level any safe harbor or ally Humans First has. An attack on an ambassador is considered an attack on all of parliament."

Zasha didn't mention anything else. She could have spoken about the potential for the lower planets to join the APU—would this change Al's mind? No discussion would' change what she had to do, which was put a stop to the ships Kascade had assembled, the war he marched the galaxy towards.

"If we gather any other intelligence, we will be sure to pass it along."

Al nodded then the screen went blank.

"We can't leave him to Kascade's plans. Not Sampson, not the kid."

Zasha turned to find Lee standing in the galley entrance, leaning against the wall, arms crossed.

"I agree," Gina said, her light blinking brighter than usual.

Zasha shook her head. "No. We have to stick to the plan. There are bigger things at stake than one person. This is the whole galaxy. Mothers, fathers, children…everyone is at risk if Kascade starts this war. If we have a single chance at stopping him, it's worth taking."

Gina's light dulled a bit. "Dottie says she is ready to start work on those components."

Zasha downed the rest of her coffee and moved to the sink.

Lee called out, loud and clear, "I think this plan was a bad idea, and we should have stuck with Sampson. If he'd had Gina's firepower of to back him up, maybe things wouldn't have gone the way they did."

Scrubbing the cup, Zasha contemplated her next words. She needed the assassin on her side, not working against her. "I don't disagree with you, but I think we have come too far down this road to make changes now. I say we stick to the plan, and if we're still alive at the end, we can rescue Sampson."

Zasha turned only to see Lee shaking her head. "That's not how we've operated as a team in the past. We don't leave people behind."

"I understand, but he knew the risks when he left. You can't tell me Sampson didn't already account for them." Zasha left the room and headed to the workspace in the cargo bay, something Sampson had created and set up. Even as she walked towards Dottie and the awaiting task, her thoughts were still on him.

He'd left without saying goodbye. *Wouldn't you?*

She'd mulled over his lack of communicating multiple times and compared it to her own abrupt departures. Even when she'd betrayed Sampson and his crew, she'd left him a message, given him some reason for what she'd done at the risk of her heart.

And he'd failed to do the same.

That was how she was able to keep heading to the cargo bay and not give orders to Gina to track Sampson down straight away.

She made it to the worktable still strong in her convictions.

"Been waiting for you. Heard Sampson was captured." Dottie flipped up the eye cover on her protection helmet and offered Zasha a soldering kit.

"Gina tell you?"

Dottie nodded, flipped the visor back down and went back to work matching the appropriate wirings.

Zasha grabbed a protection helmet of her own and followed Dottie's path sealing the ends together. It took a few minutes. She checked the connections again, ensuring everything was in place.

Once complete, she sighed. "One down."

Dottie moved the visor up again. "Only ten more to go. You're not bad at this. Ever give consideration to working more on the engineering side of things? I mean, my knowledge is not that extensive, but you seem to have talent like Sampson."

Zasha contemplated the idea, being like Sampson. She'd tried so hard and all it had won her was losing him again anyway. Their goals didn't line up and she wasn't the type to sit in the background when work needed to be done, changes made.

"I might be good at it, but in this galaxy, people can't be good at one thing only."

Dottie grinned. "You're right. Let's finish this."

They kept grinding, connecting the proper wires, soldering them until each chip sat perfectly assembled.

"Gina, what do you think?" Zasha asked because of course the AI had tracked their progress, and if Gina had seen an error, she would have spoken up sooner than later.

"Everything appears accurate, and this will ensure I can merge to one of the synth bodies."

Dottie frowned as she removed the protective helmet. "Will you be able to get back in the ship if something goes wrong?"

"There's a forty percent chance I won't be able to return, dependent on the safeguards built into the body itself. There are reasons synths are so new, and I would estimate they are locked down from outside influences or connecting networks."

It was already disconcerting enough to have a ship able to hack into systems using satellite connections and limited data networks. If an AI inside a body could do the same... The possibilities were harmful to anyone with power.

Especially if their loyalties were uncertain and anyone could reprogram something connected to a network, just had to possess the right—

"Zasha, is there a problem?"

"Hmm?"

Gina's light blinked. "You had this far-off look in your eye, and your focus and concentration stunted. Is there a problem?"

Zasha shook her head. "Not at all. Thinking about the mission."

"You're worried about Sampson," Dottie supplied.

Zasha latched on to the comment like a support tether. "Yes, and he should be here, be part of this. Most likely he's being tortured instead."

Dottie dropped the tool in her hand, and it clattered to the floor. "I don't want to contemplate such a thing."

Neither did Zasha, but the possibility remained the most likely. Knowing what she did about Kascade now made her believe the darker natures of the mercs were as possible with Humans First as they had been with the guild.

The only real question was if he was worth enough to Kascade to keep alive.

Gina's light blinked. "I have new information about Sampson based on the tracking communications. He's on Mars and is at the Smiths' compound."

Chapter Seventeen

Sampson hated small, cramped spaces, especially on ships where bone powder and liquid waste blended. But compared to this damn hole, anywhere on ship would be a luxurious adventure.

Hours, days, they blended together. Even after Sampson had agreed to help Kascade, the bastard had sealed up the hole and left him. He could vaguely make out the evening hours, when things above would get loud. Boisterous music, stomping of feet and sometimes booze leaking through the boards.

He'd attempted to sip from the leaky floorboards once, and almost coughed a lung up. The cheap corn shine burned his throat, sharp not sweet, like some sort of pure alcohol mess not designed for regular human consumption.

Those people should be dead.

Regardless, two rounds of rowdy stomping and partying had come and gone. If he went by those measures, two days had passed. Would Gina be coming soon?

Sampson silently cursed at himself for not having even bothered to look at Gina and Zasha's plan before he'd left. No, he'd been too hurt to bother with it, frustrated still at their goals being so opposite and how Zasha had refused to compromise. They could have been together. Returned the Smith's son then gone after Kascade...if he'd wanted to get involved.

Honestly, if she had been with him, if they had been on *Gina* —

"A bunch of ifs don't make reality." Speaking out loud, his voice all cracked and hoarse, made the despair a little more real.

Sampson began to consider Kascade didn't need him at all, that he only wanted to see if he could break Sampson. But Sampson was far from broken. He'd learned at least one thing in his life working for bad people — the only way out meant getting involved.

A soft thud sounded above him, followed by the scrape of wood and screech of metal.

Then illumination. The hole flooded with bright light.

"Heads up." A male voice called down, as a rope ladder rolled into view from the hole entrance.

Sampson grabbed for it and gave a couple of tugs, because *don't trust the first possible lifeline thrown to you.* Emilio had said those words once or twice.

When he confirmed the rope was secure, Sampson started to climb. The hellacious effort made his already sore muscles burn and easily brought attention to his bruised ribs, the aches and pains more apparent with each rung he ascended.

Finally, at the top, a proffered metal hand was granted to him and he took hold of the cold appendage. The strength of the other man was what got him out of the hole. Sampson stumbled out onto his knees and took a few deep, slow breaths. The air up here was less stale, but not sweet-smelling. From the hints of booze, piss, and sour wafting into his nose, no one had bothered to clean up after the last party.

"Need a drink?" The man who'd helped him shoved a bottle toward him.

Sampson glanced up. "No shine."

His rescuer chuckled, his blue eyes filled with mirth. This guy was all blond hair, scruffy face, and tan skin, except for the cybernetic arm, and appeared to find situations like this funny. "It's not shine. It's water."

Sampson's reaction of jerking the bottle out of blondie's remaining human hand and downing it brought more laughter from his would-be rescuer.

"After you're finished with that, I'll help you to the back room. Get you cleaned up before Bebe comes to take you to the shipyard."

"Who the hell are you?" Sampson didn't remember this guy's face from his last visit to the town, and he never forgot any of the faces who betrayed his entire crew and who'd threatened Toni and Emilio. Bebe Smith sat at the top of the list.

"I'm Drag, and you?" He still crouched by Sampson's side, his arms out cautiously.

Resting the water bottle against his lower lip, he replied, "I'm Sampson. That's a helluva name."

"It's my racer handle, but everyone calls me that. Real names don't count on this planet. Came over from the McIntosh gang about a year ago. Smith needed a new racer after one of their guys got banged up, and I needed to get away from a crap situation. Trying to level the playing field."

Sampson downed the rest of the water and thrust the bottle back towards Drag. "Yeah, but you aren't afraid to get involved in the dirtier aspects of the gig, it seems."

Drag frowned but took the bottle and went over to a big drum, where he stuck the container under the spigot and started to refill it. "Hey, I have no clue what the hell you were put down there for. Most people get shoved in the hole for starting bar fights and crap. Some spy on our racers and are engineers. Sometimes I get the luxurious duty of dragging out those who get thrown in. All the yard dogs get the assignment from time to time.

"So, don't lump me in with whoever threw you in there or what you did to deserve it. I got nothing to do with any crap. I'm just a guy who collects his paycheck and for a few extra duties here and there—nothing illegal, mind you—I get free room and board."

Drag crossed back over to him and handed him the bottle, which Sampson took without hesitation. He was so damn thirsty.

"How long have I been in there?"

Drag shrugged. "Your guess is as good as mine. I got back from a supply run this morning, left a couple days ago. Picking up fuel and some parts on trade, so had to be sometime after I left."

Sampson watched Drag suspiciously, trying to gauge if the man told the truth or not. Of course, the blond idiot didn't have a reason to lie, unless he was supposed to spy on Sampson, to try to get him to start talking about *Gina* and his crew.

He can die waiting.

"Well then, where's this wash-up room?"

Thirty minutes later, Sampson sat in a chair, washed, his bruised ribs bandaged, with clean clothes and salve provided for the cuts and bruises on his face.

Drag whistled low. "Clean up real nice. I think you're presentable now, but Bebe will give the final word. She doesn't like anyone looking like trash. Not representing the gang."

"She doesn't like this being called a gang either. Why do you think I'm going to be working for Bebe?" Sampson finished rubbing the salve into what felt like a bruise on his upper cheek.

"Why else would you be alive?"

Drag's assessment made sense. Sampson imagined even if the racer didn't dirty his hands, he still had inside knowledge of how the gang worked, including the number of dead bodies left lying around.

"Do you know anything about this Kascade guy Bebe is aligned with?"

Drag opened his mouth to say something, but snapped it shut as the door to the wash area creaked open.

"Drag, is he ready yet? We have things needing done." Bebe stuck her head inside, her bleach-blonde hair done up in matching braids, her bosom thrust upward by some black leather corset and the tops of her breasts on display. The woman was aware of her assets and smiled when Sampson naturally glanced.

"Looks like you clean up nice."

Drag smiled and nodded. "That's what I told him."

Bebe's smile faded and she glanced at Drag. "Get back to the racer warehouse. I'll take things from here. Snapper is needing you. Has some questions about those parts you brought back."

"Shit. Well, later. Hell, man, good luck." Drag thrust his hand out toward Sampson. This guy was too friendly for his own good. It made a man wonder what type of person he'd be when they asked him not to be nice.

"Same to you." He reluctantly embraced Drag's palm. The two shook then Drag left without a backward glance.

"He's a sweetheart, isn't he?" Bebe asked, ogling Drag's ass as he walked out and towards the front door of the bar.

"Makes a good first impression, but I imagine he's hiding things like everyone else on this damn planet."

Bebe turned back at Sampson and grinned. "You're right to be suspicious, but I imagine being around my daughter, she helped cultivate that in you. How is she?"

He answered as honestly as he could. "I don't know. Haven't seen her in almost a month. Could be dead."

Bebe's motioned for him to come towards her. "I don't like your tone. You got that from her, too. Follow me. I'll take you to the shipyard and don't even think about trying to get the drop on me. I have a guard here and an extra outside. You'll follow through on your word or you'll be shot dead."

As Sampson crossed the threshold, he caught a glimpse of a hulk of a man standing there. This time there was more light available, and he recognized the idiot as the guy who had tried to cause a scuffle between Toni and Emilio on his last visit to Mars.

Outside the building, the second buffed-up guard joined them. Bebe offered Sampson a scarf. Though it wouldn't do much, he wrapped it around his mouth and nose and covered his eyes with a pair of sun goggles.

The red planet was...red. Bright red, with the sunlight not being absorbed so much as reflecting off it. The terraforming operation here hadn't worked as well. So, Mars made do. They still mined, they still hauled ore and built ships and racers, a manufacturing planet with red dust kicked up consistently by the winds or the racers moving around.

They reached the shipyard after about ten minutes of walking. The big building with the surrounding fence sat on the far side of the town...town being a single street with about ten to fifteen buildings, some businesses and some homes. The gang was dispersed between these and worked in either the racing warehouse or the shipping one.

But this shipyard appeared far more equipped than Sampson had seen on his last visit to the crappy town of Frog Lick. Over twenty ships were stored here, covered in big sheets of various colored tarp stitched together. Instead of heading for the ships, Bebe brought him to the big building, a metal structure large enough to handle assembly of the ships before being moved into the yard.

Sure enough, inside he could see the welding torches, their sparks and the heat adding to the already oppressive air. Additional noise came from dripping water and shouts of men asking for a part or to move heavy machinery.

They kept moving to the far wall, then up two flights of stairs. At the end of a steel platform stood a double-bolted metal door. A knock then the door hissed as the bolts pulled back.

So much for getting the fatch out of here.

"Head in there. Kascade is waiting for you." Bebe stepped out of the way and let him pass. "Don't do anything stupid. I'd hate to tell my daughter you died being dumb."

Kascade turned as Sampson entered, a cocky grin emerging on his face. A closer look showed scars and the gray streaks were now more prominent in his shoulder-length hair. The smile failed to wipe away the coldness in his eyes.

How could Zasha be inspired by this?

"Sampson, you have finally come to join me. I hope your time to think proved fruitful."

What the fatch? Time to think? Sampson had been left battered, bruised and starved. His stomach grumbled again in protest.

"Hungry?" Kascade pointed to a plate with some sort of sandwich on it. "You're welcome to this and whatever else you'd like. I'm sure Bebe's people can get something."

Sampson hesitated, but only for two seconds. His stomach refused to be picky. Even if the food were poisoned, he'd reached the point of no longer caring. He took one bite and almost moaned at the taste of meat and cheese, the small crunch of grain from the bread not the best quality. But who cared? *Not me.*

A bottle of water sat next to the plate, and without asking, Sampson picked it up and downed half the contents in a single swallow.

"Ah, yes." Kascade hummed in approval. "Meditation and fasting can bring a man low. Are you ready to begin work?"

Sampson nodded because the words weren't coming with the food stuffed in his hole.

"Good. All of these computers contain the software I've programmed these ships with and the AI's programming. I need to add a deeply embedded self-destruct sequence the synths will be unaware of and that only I will have access to through this box." Kascade, the insane terrorist, held up a small handheld device with a screen and two buttons.

Sampson swallowed the last of the sandwich. "You want to destroy everything you built?"

"I want the option to destroy it."

A little over the top. "I can't build something so complex...at least not so the synths won't find it. AIs are programmed to know any and all things about their ships."

In under two seconds, Kascade went from smiling and calm to deadly grimace with a gun cocked and pointed at Sampson's head. The other two people in the room both chuckled. One a woman, and the other...the very bastard who had been on Saturn stealing the Smiths' kid.

"Then I have no use for you. Bebe said you're the best, but if not, then you die here."

Sampson saw his life flash before his eyes and the only thing he snagged on was the idea of never seeing Zasha again. He held up his hands. "Wait. Walk me through this again."

* * * *

All the pieces were in place. Now they needed to head for Mars. The fact Kascade held Sampson made the plans for his rescue simpler in her mind.

They'd taken off from the moon a day prior, moving into position and maintaining a short distance from

Mars within six to eight hours. This allowed Gina to monitor any communications going off planet.

"Anything?" Zasha asked as she entered the command deck.

Dottie shook her head as she stood, then stretched. "Nope. I'm headed for bed. A few hours would do me good. Your turn to be on watch now."

"Gina?" Zasha took up position in Dottie's chair, oddly enjoying the warmth left by the other woman. Space was damn cold. Being on the moon, stationary, had spoiled her. Or maybe it was the lack of Sampson's body heat. She hadn't been cold in his quarters.

Please be alive.

"Yes, I am monitoring transmissions. Nothing of interest, mainly racing requests, trades for parts. Personal communications. Why do men talk this way to each other, Zasha?"

Zasha brought her coffee mug to her lips. She let the hot liquid serve as another warming method. "What do you mean?"

"One message from Drag to someone named Zealot. He calls him a piece of worm larvae and if he doesn't fix the error on the parts trade, he'll spill his intestines over the track before the next race."

Zasha almost spit up her coffee but kept it down. She sat up in her chair. "It's trash talk. Everyone does it."

"Everyone?"

"Haven't you heard Emilio and Toni or even Lee? Everyone says things about people to either show them they're serious or when they joke around."

Gina's light blinked green, then blue. "I recall some of this, and Sampson has explained before, but my understanding is 'trash talk' stayed among friends only."

"Enemies too. Anything else?"

Should Gina even get a body without knowing the intricacies of how humanity worked? Trading insults was as common as bodies or bone powder.

"No, but I have found some interesting satellite surveillance which I've used to pinpoint where Kascade is building his ships." Gina pulled up the imagery on the holo-screen. "There are at least twenty ships in this yard, and they weren't there before."

"How would you know?"

"Because Frog Lick is my mother's town, and Gina's been there before."

The female voice behind her made Zasha jump, and she pivoted fast, dropping her mug to the floor as she pulled her gun from the holster strapped to her hip.

"How did you get here?"

Toni Morales smiled big, flashing near-perfect teeth. "Is that any way to greet someone you once tried to kill?"

* * * *

Zasha leaned against the far wall of the command deck, trying to decide how pissed she was at Gina. Gina, who'd let the Morales' and Smiths board as soon as they'd signaled.

The group of four appeared more focused not on the plan to stop Kascade, but on saving Jace and Sampson.

"You're mad at me?" Gina asked, her voice focused to the light bar right next to Zasha, instead of the entire room.

Zasha huffed. "Wouldn't you be?"

"I don't experience emotions, but I can detect elevated blood pressure. So yes, you're mad. You have cause, but even though I am with you on this plan, in some ways for my own reasons, I know Sampson must be saved."

"Why do you care?" The damn ship hadn't appeared to care when the news first came in or had she?

"He saved me. I owe him the biggest debt or else I would have never become what I am today. We can still do this, our plan. We leave the others to rescue Sampson and the child."

"Hey," Emilio called over to Zasha, "no private conversations with my ship. Get over here, and you both start talking. Because what I am seeing here means problems for me when it's all over."

Fatch. Emilio wouldn't want to risk losing his ship. Without the AI in place, this vessel would require a slightly larger crew, plus major adjustments. Gina ran everything, even the coffee machine.

"What's the concern?" Zasha asked, moving closer. All eyes were on her, four pairs staring at her with the kind of distrust she'd experienced for most of her life. As a mercenary, stares of displeasure came with the territory and she missed Sampson...who'd found a way to gaze at her as if she were special.

"You're going to put my AI into a synth. My ship will be exposed, and we could lose Gina entirely." Emilio slammed his hand against the table, the holo-screen rattling. "Whose damn idea was this, and why didn't Sampson stop it?"

"It's mine," Gina confessed. "I wouldn't let him stop me."

Toni's eyes went wide, along with Loyda's. Emilio's scowl looked like it could cut glass.

Al laughed. "This is rich, that boy has made the AI curious for life. Take it from me, humanity isn't worth it. Better to keep to the ship."

Gina's light turned yellow — frustration. "Is it? You love your wife, your child, Alexander Smith?"

Al frowned. "Yes."

"Same for Emilio loving Toni, for Sampson loving Zasha."

All eyes came back to her, burning Zasha with their judgment or surprise. She hated being the center of attention, hated having her and Sampson's feelings on display.

"I want the same. I want to know what love and desire feel like, and being in a ship won't get me any closer."

Emilio sighed. "Being a synth might not either. You can't know what to expect, what will happen. Zasha's plan also outlines trying to stop a mad man from launching ships, and you're more focused on a body. I think this affects your success rates."

Zasha spoke up then. "We all have different goals, but the end result is the same. Stop a potential war, save our loved ones and live our best lives. How we go about getting to the final result may be slightly different for each of us."

Loyda came closer to Zasha. "Then you'll save Sampson."

"I can't. My battle is against Kascade. Taking down these ships. I need this group to help with the saving department. I'm not good at keeping things alive, only killing them." The honest truth, the confession she'd kept to herself all these years.

"She's right," Toni agreed. "Her skill set is about dismantling. I think we can take care of the protecting piece."

If they're alive.

Zasha didn't voice her worst fears. This was what happened to her every time — the things she loved the most were ripped from her. She'd pushed Sampson away due to her desire to get him aligned to her plans, instead of finding a compromise. She had decided to pursue her own goals no matter the cost, though if they'd talked after the last time...

What if I never get the chance to choose him?

Ultimately, she couldn't now, not when she had to stop Kascade.

"Then if we're going to be the rescue team, what do we do?" Emilio asked.

Lee cleared her throat. The assassin had arrived at some point and stood near the entrance to command as if waiting for her moment. "I have an idea."

Chapter Eighteen

Sampson struggled with Kascade's requirements. The ship software and AI work already impressed him. Judging from what little he'd learned on the moon base, the moonies themselves had put together the bulk of this without even realizing what it would be used for.

From the amount of code, to the safety features, the AIs created here were probably more sophisticated than Gina, meaning it would take twice as long to understand the intricacies. *Time I don't have.*

"Two solar days," Kascade said. It seemed the guy possessed an affinity for the number two. "I have a meeting then and need to be ready for a show of force."

"Easy, show off the big fleet of ships," Sampson mumbled as Kascade left the room. The sass earned him a smack from one of the seconds in command, Tia. What she lacked in height, she made up for by being lightning quick. If he didn't know better, he'd almost believe Lee had a twin, but one who fancied their face up with beauty products and had shorter hair.

"Work faster," she repeated.

He tried — Karma be damned — he tried. He was never allowed to leave the room, relegated to a tiny closet with a pot as a toilet. Food, a small amount of it along with water, got brought in three times that day, though they expected him to eat and work at the same time.

Sleep? What is sleep? He'd been working for over fifteen hours and finally threw his hands in the air.

"I'm done. I need rest. Shoot me if you want, but at this point if I don't sleep, I won't be getting this done anyway."

Tia eyed him with suspicion. Then she reached into a small compartment in the floor and pulled out a couple of blankets and a pillow. She tossed them at him. "Then sleep. You have five hours."

"Five, that's it?"

She lifted her gun and took the safety off. "Take the five or take death."

"At least I know how extreme you people are about rest periods. Jeez, calm your barrel, lady." Sampson snuggled up with the blankets and the pillow as best he could, first in a chair and finally on the floor, so he could spread out.

He dreamed of one woman and being held in her arms.

* * * *

The five hours were gone in a flash, but they did the trick. He finally understood how to build in the self-destruct code. To master the sequence so each ship would have identical commands, and they would be controlled with the push of one button.

It had seemed impossible, but now...not so much.

My big fatching brain. Yep, it will work.

Tia appeared interested in watching his progress as his fingers flew across the keyboards, splicing codes and merging the information to put ultimate destruction in her leader's hands.

"Have you discovered the solution?"

Sampson nodded. "Uh-huh, now to finalize it."

And build in my own safeguard because no one needs this much power. The circuit control inside the handheld box proved a bit more complicated to build and upload the commands into. He ran multiple simulations, the only way to test the damn thing. Finally, Sampson stood, screwed on the front of the box and connected the power source.

"You can tell Kascade it's ready."

Sampson expected to be put back in the hole or left in the room. Maybe Tia would even shoot him. Nothing existed outside the realm of possibility when dealing with mad men.

Instead, Tia sent a communication via some handheld holo-screen. She marched over to him once she received a response. "Grab the box and come with me."

The button to unlock the door let out a deep tone, and they walked out of the software office, down the stairs. The noises from the previous days had gone silent, no more welding or water dripping. No shouts paired with the strange sounds of whining metal. Instead, a fully complete ship, as big as Gina, sat inside the warehouse.

Tia marched him around to the back and they hustled up a loading ramp into a cargo area. "Follow me to the command deck and remain silent, or I'll shoot you."

He was a fool mesmerized by the ship itself and the engineering. The tinkering side of him had wanted to see every last seal and rivet.

Should have tried to escape.

He'd had the opportunity since only Tia served as his escort from the software room to here. Unfortunately, now there were other guards. Multiple men with weapons, in merc garb, and almost all of them sported the Humans First tattoo.

"Hey, Tia. Boss said no one goes in or out." This from some goon in an outfit that looked ridiculous more than anything, with bright colored strips of leather fastened into a vest, along with two big guns strapped across his chest and red grav boots. The man was a walking target screaming 'shoot me first.'

"I have other instructions. Back off, mercenary," Tia growled.

So not all remained happy with this arrangement, not everyone completely loyal.

That could work to my favor.

Once past the guards lining the cargo bay, they went down a long hallway. Voices rose, filled with frustration and anger, but Kascade's boomed above them all, urging them to silence.

"We walk in, and you will hand Kascade the box, understand?" Tia glanced over her shoulder, expecting nothing less than complete compliance. He'd created this false sense of loyalty and he'd maintain his fake complacency for now.

Sampson glanced at the device in his hand, small, square and capable of a lot of murder. The war-starting kind. "Have those ships launched?"

"Yes," Tia replied in a harsh whisper. "Now, do as instructed."

The door slid open, and Sampson walked in. The scene before him wasn't what he'd expected. There were no people in the room except Kascade and his other second, Darren. Darren who held a barely coherent Jace.

Fatching hell.

The holo-table in front of them showed multiple people, people he didn't recognize save for one. Big Al Smith.

"Ambassadors of the APU, as stated before, this is not a negotiation. This is a surrender. You will cease to plague the lower planets with your demands for our technology, our ships or anything for that matter. We will not submit to your rule or subjugation. Anything you have we want can be bartered for, at fair price…no longer taken."

Tia nudged Sampson on the shoulder. "Take it to him."

The box could fatching wait—this man had declared open war on the APU and the upper planets.

"The people on the lower planets won't survive," Al countered.

Kascade laughed. "You foolishly believe this, but we will. We can turn all our focus on ourselves instead of settling for the upper's scraps. If you won't answer to our initial demand, you will answer to this."

The terrorist pointed at Jace. "We can take your children, the same way you have taken ours for hundreds of years. No more will you exploit our bodies or future. We will find a way to be self-sustaining."

Al growled. "You touch my son and I'll kill you."

"I believe you are too far away to follow through on such a threat." Kascade turned and spied Sampson, then smiled. "Ah, yes...come here, Sampson."

He walked forward more out of dread than anything. Death hovered over him like the gravitational pull of a black hole, ready to suck him in. No way he would get out of this alive, but still his legs moved, as if any action were better than standing still. His brain raced with thoughts, seeking a way to escape.

When he reached the bottom of the steps and crossed to Kascade's side, the older man held out his hand. Sampson, on autopilot, extended the box.

Al's frustration was visible in his crossed arms and fearsome frown. "What's the meaning of this? Kascade, we don't care about your friend here. The other planets aren't in line with your will to start a war."

Kascade closed his hand around the box, and Sampson found it difficult to let go. Finally, with a harder pull, and push to Sampson's shoulder, the box was released from his hold and now in the hands of a psycho.

"There won't be a war. If you don't agree to concede the lower planets from the APU and to remove your presence from past the asteroid belt, my ships are on slip stream currents to all major cities on the upper planets will self-destruct."

"A move of aggression will erase your army," one of the other ambassadors said.

"Suicide," chimed another.

Kascade shrugged. "Possibly so, but I'll take yours with mine. Make no mistake, the losses will be large, but with no more access to Mars to facilitate your ships, no moon tech to equip those ships, who can rebuild faster?"

Horrifying.

The clench of Sampson's stomach, his chest and entire body, grew tense at the implications of what he had created. Then, in a moment of clarity, he stumbled to get back to the door. His rush to remove himself from the room was cut short when the power went out.

Backup generators roared to life as the command deck doors opened. The following explosion sent Tia flying through the air. Sampson dropped to the floor to avoid debris, covering his head with his hands. Not the smartest decision, but it worked.

When he dared to look up, a goddess walked in, all long legs encased in black pants, blonde ponytail swinging and a gleam in her purple eyes.

"Sampson, get up." The voice and tone were eerie and recognizable.

He scrambled to his feet. "Gina, what the hell?"

"We're rescuing you." This came not from Gina, but Lee, whose moment got cut off as Tia ran at her with a battle cry.

More voices scrambled behind them, but Sampson started glancing around for Darren and Jace. The sound of feet running, guns cocking never fazed him—this was what he'd grown used to over the years of being with Toni and Emilio. Danger should have been his middle name.

"Gina, do you see Darren?"

"Huddled in the corner." The smoke in the room reduced the visibility, but Sampson crouched and could tell from the boots on the floor where the fool tried to hide. Sampson moved fast, hustling low to the ground. With a thrust from the balls of his feet, he launched up and punched Darren in the face multiple times. A right hook, a left jab...all while the hulk held Jace in his arms.

To Sampson's dismay, the thrown fists didn't seem to faze the larger man. *Fatch*.

Darren's steely-eyed stare met Sampson's and the goon returned the hits to Sampson's face, knocking him down.

There was a flash of light as an object flew through the air, the glint of metal and the sharp pole-like cylinder impaling Darren through the center of his head with enough force to lodge him into the wall. Jace cried out—Darren's tight grip was on the kid, who jostled in his hold. Sampson moved quickly to remove Jace from the dead man's embrace and keep himself from gagging at the same time.

Sure, he'd killed a man or two before, but the gore here was more visible with bits of brain matter, blood and skin scattered.

Jace whimpered, his face bearing remnants of Darren. Sampson wiped them off the best he could with his sleeve. They needed Doc, but Sampson didn't see the medical expert in the room. The holo-screen had gone dead. Gina fought with bastards at the door, and Lee appeared to have the upper hand over Tia.

"Gina, we need to get out of here," Sampson hollered.

The only problem...no Kascade. Where did the bastard go?

"I'll have a clear path within five seconds. Be ready to head into the corridor but go left—don't head back to the cargo bay," Gina yelled.

Sampson followed the directions and headed out of command. He had no clue where he was going, but with Jace tucked close to his chest, he kept moving and hoped for an exit. Gina had never steered him wrong before. Suddenly, he saw Zasha's head.

A million different emotions flooded his body, relief, fear, happiness…the woman he loved was less than thirty steps away.

"Zasha?"

"Sampson, here. Get ready to duck down into this hole." Zasha's head disappeared, and Sampson followed her through the hatch in the floor, down a ladder and into the ship warehouse.

He wanted to ask what the hell but didn't get a chance as Zasha clamped her hand over Sampson's mouth.

"You have questions, but we don't have time. When I let go of your mouth run for the shuttle over there." She pointed to a side door where only darkness waited.

She let go of his mouth, and he caught sight of Gina and Lee coming down the ladder.

"Zasha —"

"There's no time."

They all took off running. Shouts sounded behind them. Sampson heard gunfire but ignored the possible threat. He kept moving, filled with renewed hope and the idea that somehow, they would all get out of here alive. The shuttle entrance on the other side of the door materialized, and they piled in. Sampson turned around as Gina moved past him to the pilot's seat, Lee following. Except, no Zasha.

She was right behind me.

Sampson went to the door, and there she ran, chasing after something. Off in the distance he caught sight of what had slowed her down. Kascade, running away, with his remaining guards offering protection.

She turned back to glance at him, hesitation in her eyes, then came to a stop.

He shook his head and motioned for her to come back, and she did.

For a moment, the relief swamped him as she returned to his side, threatening to overwhelm his senses. She came to a halt, her body brushing against his. The kid between them stopped them from closing the remaining distance.

"I love you," she said before she pressed her lips against his. He tried to deepen the kiss and for a moment she let him.

Then she shoved him backward and pressed the button inside the door to close the hatch on the shuttle. Instinctively, he wrapped his free hand around Jace's head to secure the kid.

He regained equilibrium fast, attempting to open the hatch and hold on to Jace, but the seal refused to budge. "Gina, let me out. Open the door!"

The shuttle took off.

"Sorry, Sampson. We are out of time."

* * * *

Zasha sprinted after the man who'd lied to her. Chasing Kascade across a Mars shipping warehouse wasn't part of what they'd discussed prior to rescuing Sampson. But honestly, when did plans work out? Originally, they'd been supposed to stop the fleet.

Originally, she should have confronted Kascade before he called a meeting with APU representatives.

None of their carefully devised options had worked out. No, they'd caught the last ship before launch, Gina invading the synth pilot while Emilio, Toni and the rest had commandeered the ship to track some of the vessels, leaving Al and Loyda on *Gina* to wait for the rescue group.

Zasha had no clue if they would be successful at stopping Kascade's fleet, but if she could stop the man himself, the attack and would-be war would end.

Chasing him brought her to a set of stairs leading downward, below the surface. Narrow and metal — anyone would hear her coming.

Fatch it.

She went in with a single gun drawn, though she'd arrived more equipped. Once she'd committed to chasing Kascade, the ruthless side of her kicked in, like flipping a switch, and all the parts of herself she'd locked away now roared back to life. Noises, sights, the slightest hint of movement — she was aware of it all. She reached the bottom of the stairwell and heard rustling straight ahead. A double-thick steel door at the end of the hallway creaked and bellowed as it started to slide closed.

She grabbed her knives, aimed and fired. Cries of pain echoed down the corridor as the blades found their mark. *The idiot's wrists, hopefully.* She was encouraged by the fact that the door squeaked to a halt. Picking up pace, she made it to the opening and squeezed inside.

Another bodyguard moved toward her, preparing to fire, but his hesitation gave her time to use ol' limp wrists' body as a shield.

The bullets ravaged her human shield, and if the piss-poor excuse for a merc wasn't dead from the loss of blood due to her blades, he no longer drew breath by the time the last bullet had been fired.

She dropped the body while the guard in front of her tried to reload, and moved in close, snapping his leg then his neck. There was no time to waste as a couple of additional hired guns came toward them out of the corridor.

This time she used her weapon. Three shots and three dead bodies, the motions like second nature, muscle memory summoned forth. She wasn't proud of taking lives, but thankful she could keep herself safe. Then she saw Kascade.

"Zasha!" He roared, twin blades, one in each hand, raised. His face was red, his teeth clamped in a grimace as he started to charge her.

Her gun still had bullets, but she wanted him to pay with more than a quick death. Tucking her gun back into her holster, she prepared for his approach. She let loose with flying fists, kicks and reacted without hesitation, disarming him of his weapons though the war for the upper hand dragged on.

For a moony, Kascade was surprisingly adept at hand-to-hand combat, and he produced a new knife out of nowhere. She blocked his downward strike, whipping her hand around his, circling. It would have looked like some strange dance move but, keeping track of the blade, she maneuvered in and around his arm with ease.

As his frustration grew, the swings of the blade became wilder, less controlled, and that was when she struck. Turning his momentum against him, she grabbed the blade and plunged the sharp instrument into his upper thigh.

Kascade screamed, his injured leg sending him to the ground. Zasha circled his body and brought his hands around his back, securing them with a piece of rope from her belt. Then the holo-screen against the wall, a giant thing covering the length of the concrete space, illuminated.

The room appeared to be some sort of safety bunker, a place for Kascade to hide as he executed his terror strikes against the upper planets, innocents at his mercy.

"Kascade." Al's voice and image appeared. He looked much more at ease than when Zasha had last seen him. "It's over."

She yanked on Kascade's hair, forcing his head up so he would have to look. "Hear that, you con man. Ambassador, I have secured him. He can't do anything here."

Kascade laughed beneath her. "Oh, I can do much."

Then, with an amazing feat of strength, he threw her off him and broke the ties on the rope. Zasha lay there dazed and shook her head, attempting to clear the fuzziness.

"Halt. Kascade. Your ship fleet is no more. They're under APU control. No deal will be struck today but your surrender."

Kascade reached into his belt, and Zasha moved for her gun. She wasn't supposed to kill him, but she would.

"Not while I have this." He held aloft a small box. "Tell them what it is, Sampson."

Sampson? Her lover stepped forward into the holo-screen, clearly visible and no longer with a wide-eyed gaze. "I've already told them, and your self-destruct box is useless. Especially since I deactivated the coding."

"No. It's not." Kascade pressed the button, and nothing happened. He pressed it again and again, his anger and voice rising with frustration with each subsequent press on the worthless piece of tech. Then his gaze swung towards her.

"Fine, then your friend will be my sacrifice for your failure." He stalked toward her and she gave her best imitation of scared, scrambling backwards as if trying to get away, but really, she'd been ready for this moment the minute she saw the communication stating he was responsible for attacking the moon compound. She wanted to take the shot, to kill him. She'd do the universe a favor.

"He has to pay, Zasha." Sampson's voice cut through her musings.

She stopped moving, grabbed the gun, aimed, and fired.

Kascade fell to the ground, screaming in agony, the only sign he was alive. "You fatching bitch!"

"Zasha?" Sampson's face crowded out all the other faces in the holo-screen.

"I'm here." And exhausted. She lay back against the floor taking a moment, even as Kascade continue to howl in agony.

Sampson's voice cut through Kascade's noise, "Hold on, Zasha. We're coming to get you."

* * * *

"Hey, wake up." Sampson's voice brought her out of her slumber.

She jumped, and his arms tightened around her body until she stilled. "Where's Kascade?"

"Moving him to an APU ship. They're rounding up the other members of Humans First on planet and the Smiths."

"Smiths?" Zasha was confused. "Al and Loyda didn't do anything."

Sampson shook his head. "Not the ambassadors, but Al and Toni's mom, Bebe, and some of her men. They were involved in this too. Deeply involved. The town of Frog Lick may never recover."

Shit. "Sounds awful. I mean, our parents weren't the greatest, but kidnapping your own grandkid..."

"Yeah, we're gonna get you out of here and get some medical attention."

"I'm fine," Zasha mumbled. Her limbs and upper chest were numb in some places, sore in others.

"You're bleeding from your arm and there's blood on your torso." Sampson pointed to the two spots and she looked at them.

"Fatch, bastard must have got me, and I never noticed."

"You're unstoppable when you're on the warpath," Sampson said as he helped her to her feet.

Then he picked her up in his arms.

"Whoa there, bad boy. I think I can walk by myself. I'm not in distress." Zasha half-heartedly struggled against him.

"I'll put you down when I get you to the shuttle. These stairs might hurt those wounds and cause more bleeding."

She smiled and snuggled in close to his chest, resting her head against his warmth and listening to his heartbeat. She didn't know what would happen the next day or the next month, but for now she'd do whatever it took to stay as close to him as possible. So fine, he wanted to carry her...he could walk her across the planet.

They made it to the shuttle, with minimum additional injury. Back on *Gina*, they met up with Loyda, Al, Doc, Lee and the newly bodied Gina. Zasha faded in and out but became pretty alert with the shot Doc gave her.

"It's a numbing agent and jolts the system. I need you awake for when I stitch this wound together, so you can tell me if anything feels weird or off inside you. Especially with this being so close to the stomach."

Zasha groaned. "Then I'm going to live."

"Please say no," Lee called out from the doorway.

"She's gonna live. Everyone clear out...except Sampson. He can stay." Doc moved from the table to grab whatever torture devices he planned to use on her. Zasha hated medical work but would suffer this.

Sampson leaned over her and pressed a kiss to her forehead.

Anything for him.

"Sampson, when you and Zasha are feeling up to it, come talk to me. I have an opportunity for you both."

Zasha recognized this as Ambassador Al's voice, the deep command not a suggestion.

Sampson nodded agreement then looked back at her. "I'm in no rush."

She grinned as Doc moved back in with a big sharp sticker. "Neither am I."

Epilogue

Sampson typed in the final bit and pressed the button to run the projection through the simulator. Leaning back in his chair, he sighed, sending up a silent prayer to whatever good luck or religious deity existed that this would work.

"Trial number three thousand and fourteen commencing," announced the computer.

The drive spun, the chemical mixtures merged and by some miracle, the slip drive continued to operate.

Cheers went up around him.

"You did it," Terry said, coming up to pat him on the shoulder.

Sampson shook his head. "No, everyone in this room did. Now, record the results. I'll see you all tomorrow."

He grabbed his coat and moved out of the lab to head home. The corridors of the moon base lay in front of him and as he passed, people smiled, greeted him, and for once feeling needed wasn't of major importance…but they showed him how he was wanted here anyway.

Almost a year after the showdown with Kascade and his weak attempt at starting a galaxy war, Ambassador Big Al Smith had convinced parliament to grant the lowers membership in the APU, with representation.

Al took to heart what Kascade had said, regardless of the man's ultimate motives and encouraged parliament to also support the moon and its tech divisions in looking for a new fuel source. To further space travel and allow the human race to thrive and continue not to be divisive.

With these decisions, the moon itself was growing more successful. People on all three celestial objects, Moon, Mars and Earth had received unfamiliar support with vaccines and food, and additional relief efforts were underway.

Sampson let himself into the living quarters he shared with Zasha and immediately went to the holo-screen. Establishing communication took a little longer than he liked. After half a dozen minutes, Gina finally answered.

"Hello, Sampson."

He still couldn't get over his best friend in a body, with purple eyes and blonde hair. "Hello, Gina. Where's Zasha?"

"I'll patch you to her quarters. We should be there in a couple of solar hours."

Sampson sighed. The downside to their newfound lives and success meant Zasha had accepted a position as a representative from APU Parliament to the lowers, spearheading relief efforts, running aid shipments. Gina had agreed to participate for a limited time, as a payment for the body she'd kept, though her synth existence had been sworn to secrecy by all parties involved.

The efforts meant Sampson and Zasha saw each other only rarely.

"Yes, but it's been months."

Gina offered a nod. "Yes, Earth texts often mention how absence makes the heart grow fonder."

Sampson chuckled. "More desperate."

Her visage softened, and Sampson was reminded of her final trip. "Is this really the last one you'll do?"

She nodded. "I've paid the debt. I'm returning the vessel to Emilio. Of course, with the changes you already helped me make, they will be able to pilot the ship with ease. But I want to explore, to find my own way, to…"

Sampson got it—she wanted to experience humanity. "I'd almost warn you against it, but to do so would make the love I already have, the life I live, seem meaningless."

"It's not," Gina replied. "I want something similar."

"Then this would be goodbye?"

"You'll see me again, friend. Besides you're the only one I know who will listen to all my problems without complaint."

Sampson smiled. "All right then. Just don't be a stranger and communicate regularly."

"That sounds more like father words than friend words." Gina grinned, the expression a little more natural than her first attempts. Then she disappeared before more could be said, before he could offer a compliment, her image fading away while Zasha's took over. "Sampson! You couldn't wait a little longer."

"I've waited forever, it seems like, but I couldn't wait to share the news."

Zasha's eyes went wide. "It worked?"

He couldn't keep anything from her, ever. "Yes, simulation three thousand and fourteen. Left Terry and Rosh documenting, but it worked. We may have discovered an alternate fuel mixture for space travel."

Zasha let out a small whoop. "Then it looks like we have some celebrating to do when I arrive."

"I would hope so, because it's not only the day I discovered a new fuel source. It's also a special occasion."

"What?" He loved how her eyebrows scrunched up when she looked confused.

"The day we met."

"Mr. Morales...you pure romantic, you."

"I would hope so. I needed to conquer your mercenary heart."

* * * *

Zasha bolted off the ship as soon as they docked. She left the details up to Dottie and Doc. Gina wanted to offload as fast as possible to get the ship back to Eden. Doc and Dottie planned to stay on the moon. In fact, they'd asked Loyda about permanent quarters, and she was happy that they wanted to join her and Sampson.

The old crew was officially breaking up. Emilio and Toni were spending more and more time on Eden, and Gina was ready to head off to parts unknown. Lee was already on a separate humanitarian mission. Everything was changing, but from Sampson's attitude, the adjustment didn't seem to bother him.

At least I hope not.

She made it inside the door of their quarters, only to be immediately pinned against the wall.

Dropping her bag, she moaned as Sampson's lips met hers. Months had passed since they'd last been in each other's arms and the fast, hard way he initiated contact turned her on like nothing else.

Except, no way would he be leading the charge on his own. With a slip of her hands under his arms, and a tuck of her leg around his, it took no time to place him against the wall.

He grinned underneath her kiss. "I've been waiting for this."

"Then you better be ready to fuck me like you did that last night." The night he'd left her without saying goodbye, but she left that part out.

He leaned down, hooked one arm under her leg and the other around her back to lift her up.

"Ooh, you've been lifting the barrels."

He laughed again. "When you're away, it's hard to sleep."

The confession made her heart clench. She hated the idea of him struggling at all. "So, you work out?"

"It's either cardio and lifting or work in the lab all night staring at screens, which isn't healthy. Doc says they will rot your eyes."

They reached the bedroom, and he slowly put her down. She stared up at him in the low light coming from the floor light bar edging the walls of their room. A similar one was mounted at the top, but Sampson left the upper light off.

"Strip, fast," she commanded.

He immediately started to work at his pants, his feet bare on the floor.

She responded in kind, removing every last stitch and, before her panties fell, he was upon her, moving her toward the bed, hands, mouth—all of him. Everywhere. He treated her like some sort of fancy banquet in need of devouring, as if he'd starved himself in the months she'd been away and only her flesh, her sex, would sate him.

"Please tell me you plan to eat my pussy."

"I'm going to make you come on my face till it's covered."

"Fatch...hurry."

His face was between her legs, his tongue moving as if tracing a love letter over her clit. She writhed beneath him, fisting the sheets and begging. When she finally came, he delivered as promised, continuing to lick at her until another orgasm followed.

Only then did she cry out. "Stop. While I love you down there, I need you inside me."

He crawled up her body, kissing his way, paying homage to every inch of her, until finally the head of his cock nestled up against her entrance. "This is what you want?"

"Fuck me, please."

"How hard?"

She reached up, cupping his cheeks between her hands and pressed a kiss to his lips, enjoying the taste of herself remaining. "Shake the walls."

* * * *

Much later, she spooned with Sampson, relishing the deep breaths and rise of his chest against her back. *Nothing like this exists anywhere in the universe.*

"I never imagined this."

"Imagined what?" Sampson asked as he trailed a finger down her arm, chill bumps rising on her skin.

"We could find a way to be together."

Sampson pressed a kiss to her shoulder. "I didn't think so either, but then I realized any time I get with you is a blessing and I don't have to have all or nothing."

She rolled to face him. "Will this be enough?"

"It's not even a question I need to answer, but I will." He pushed up from the bed and moved over her, standing. "Give me a minute."

He quit the room. Zasha lay on her back, staring at the ceiling, the fancy skylight showing the stars above, twinkling in the far-off distance. A part of her began to fill with worry, like a bad bone powder mixture moving into a slip drive, doom impending. If Sampson was calling things quits…if this was over, she'd fall apart like a poisoned ship, oxygen shut down and survival not likely.

If Sampson couldn't do this long term, if their goals still differed so much…

Then he was back, and of course the tears already threatened, forming in the corners of her eyes.

"Zasha, why are you crying?"

"I can't… I don't want to lose this. I know we're apart half the time and it's trying, but I like helping people. You like solving problems. We're so different—"

"Shh." He held a finger to her lips, then wiped away the tears threatening to spill with his same hand. "I love the time I get with you. I wouldn't trade it for anything or jeopardize it. In the months we have been apart, I have realized what you do is important, to you and thousands of people. What I do is equally important. I believe we can continue to make this work."

Then he held up a sparkling object in his other hand. A circular shape, gleaming in the low light.

"What is that?" She reached for it, and he lifted it up higher, barely out of her reach.

"It's a gift. I made for you. This is from some parts that were obsolete on *Gina*, when we worked to refit things so the ship could operate without AI. I fashioned this bracelet together as a symbol of our past, and how we have grown into our future."

Tears arose, hot and fresh. She couldn't stop them, but this time she hugged Sampson to her, sitting up and wrapping her arms around him in a tight embrace.

"Does this mean you like it?" he asked, frozen in her grip, his arms outstretched but not holding her.

"I love it. Now hug me, damn it."

And she melted all over as he followed her commands. This was what made him equally precious to her, the fact if she asked, he did, and she would never want to abuse that again. Not after almost losing him.

She finally released him and let him slide the bracelet over her wrist. "Does this mean I have to marry you?"

Sampson shook his head. "No, it means I'm yours to do with as you will. If it's marriage you want or another sort of official bonding ceremony, I'll do it. But ultimately, I don't care as long as we're together."

"Bonding... Can it involve rope?" she replied with a wink.

Sampson grinned and leaned in close. "What did you have in mind?"

Want to see more from this author? Here's a taster for you to enjoy!

Full Throttle Cyborgs: Snap Me Up
Landra Graf

Excerpt

Wrench to the left to loosen. Wrench to the right to tighten. Gina Morales found the process interesting, like everything else human.

Who came up with the idea to tighten clockwise or loosen counterclockwise? Who came up with a clock?

Of course, she could answer these questions with her big AI brain, though completing the actions, experiencing them, meant far more than simply knowing.

A loud winding noise started at the opposite end of the bay and Gina didn't even bother to look. No, she'd tried to tell that idiot Snapper the engine wouldn't work, but he, like most male humans, believed he knew more than a woman did.

All right, that may be unfair. He believes he knows more than me. Stubborn through and through.

A small explosive blast erupted at the opposite end of the bay, the air wafting the scents of combustion and melting metal. Then the fire exhaust compression tanks hissed. This brought a different smell. Gina sniffed and got a good hint of ozone, crisp and clean, before the fans kicked in to clear out any possible toxic chemical reactions.

"Fuck!" Snapper's exclamation brought a smile to her face.

Since the first day Gina had stepped into the Full Throttle mechanics bay, Snapper had acted suspicious and rude. Though she half admired his cautious nature, it got a little old when he questioned every move she made.

Sure, she was lying to his face, but that was for her safety and security. No one could know she was the first-ever synthetic. Her AI brain had once been the software component of a ship named after her, but she'd evolved, and six months prior had discovered a madman from Earth's moon had worked with someone on Mars to create synthetic bodies. It was her chance to exceed her parameters and prove her worth to her creator.

Though becoming human had opened a whole new universe for her.

It's all new.

Snapper swore again and threw something. Gina set her wrench down and leaned up, squaring her shoulders as she approached him.

"It wouldn't have done that if you—"

"Don't say it, Gina." Snapper brought his hand up and massaged his temples, rubbing black slick all over his tan skin.

The dirt marring his face bothered her. The lack of attention to cleanliness—she itched to take care of it. Problem-solving was a natural reaction to her root programming, as it had been for more than twelve years.

"You have—"

He whirled around to face her, blue eyes blazing. "Are you finished with the engine tune-up on that hauler?"

A shit job he'd given her for daring to make a suggestion the last time. As an AI, she should have learned her lesson, and she had, but being human meant trying again. At least, Sampson had always told her that.

"I'm almost done. Just tightening the last few bolts."

"Then maybe stick to it and let me worry about the engine."

She took a deep breath. "I would be happy to, though you should know that if you added an extra row of plugs, it would be able to distribute the load more evenly."

"You're a racing engineer now, are you? Your skills were slip drives and trolling motors when you showed up. Best stick to haulers, drifters and ships, and leave the racers to us."

Gina clenched her jaw. "Snapper—"

"Gina, how about you finish your assignment and let me deal with 'ol grumpy ass here." The voice beside her belonged to Drag, the newly appointed leader of Frog Lick and the Full Throttle gang. This town and the gang used to belong to the Smiths, but they were long gone now, moved on or arrested. What was left was a blend of Smiths, others from another gang called Macintosh and some stragglers from non-affiliated gangs that had earned a place with Full Throttle.

Drag had been the one to give her chance, while his buddy Snapper wanted to give her a hard time. Where Drag was all blond hair, straight-cut and slicked-back, with a solid build and trimmed goatee, Snapper was dark, curly hair and untamed beard. Like a wild man fitting into the uncivilized stereotypes often used to describe Mars men on the upper planets.

"Aye, aye, cap…er, boss." She caught herself but didn't miss how Drag's blond eyebrow raised a fraction.

Instead of doubling down with more words that might give herself away, or cause more questions, she pivoted on her foot and went right back to the hauler. Her wrench waited for her, and she grabbed it, though her curiosity couldn't be helped. She'd always been more of a listener anyway, from her years possessing an inanimate object.

"I don't like her, Drag."

She wrenched with a little more force than planned, and the damn bolt squeaked. Her grip eased up as the conversation continued.

"You could at least hear her out. She might have a good idea or two."

Gina liked Drag. Liked him a lot. He was logical, smart, thoughtful, and he was constantly attempting to improve the gang town, in more ways than others did. Starting with equality for women and men… Prior to Drag taking over as gang leader, women weren't allowed to work in the mechanics bay or any areas of ship building and mining.

Snapper growled. "Maybe, but I don't have time for ideas right now. We needed this racer ready to start testing, we're pushing it as things are. Now, I got nothing."

"You got a body, just not an engine. It's all right, we have time, and you go back to the drawing board. We'll get thoughts from others at the town meeting tonight. Many heads are better than one."

Funny how Gina had tried to tell Snapper the same thing a couple days ago and he shot her down. Drag, on the other hand, was able to get through. At least, Snapper's weary sigh implied most of his fight was gone.

"Fine, I'll be at the meeting, though I was hoping to skip it."

"No," Drag replied. "I need you there. You and Rune are my right hands. We need to show a united front, more than ever."

Gina tightened the last bolt in place and slammed the engine cover down, doing her best to give the impression she wasn't hanging on every word...except the pair had gone silent. She glanced over and saw Snapper's pensive expression. Those fingers were back to massaging engine grease into his skin.

She rubbed her own fingertips together. The presence of grease there made her stomach turn a bit. Dirt, grime—she'd been a ship, knew the feel of such things, yet even now she ached to clean her hands.

"They turned us down, didn't they?"

Snapper's question was met by Drag's nod of agreement. *Not good at all.*

She gathered her tools and dropped them in the box against the wall. Another quick look—Drag and Snapper were now talking to their driver, Hemi. She took that moment to slip away to the sink and contemplate her next move.

The water and soap were this mash of odd sensation that she'd never get used to, though less overwhelming than the baths with the full immersion into the liquid. She'd almost frozen in fear the first time she'd cleaned herself, her experience limited to the ion showers on the ships. No water, no waste. Though here, everything was recycled, filtered, and re-used.

Soapy suds were swept clean by droplets of liquid—the same liquid that powered humanity. Seventy percent of their bodies was composed of this life-giving nectar.

Gina dried her hands on a towel and then took another peek around the corner—with Drag and Snapper sidetracked, she could log her progress on the hauler in the computer and potentially access the other files. It wouldn't take long, and this was her best chance, while the system was unlocked and available.

She hadn't dared let the machine log her as getting in after hours or attempt to erase the evidence. In other circumstances, a little light hacking might work, but one never knew when a tech might discover her digital fingerprints and cause her trouble.

Snapper's attitude towards her increased her desire to take the risk. She was tired of waiting, taking it slow, per Sampson's suggestion. Hell, Sampson didn't even know she wanted to find her maker.

Maybe Sampson didn't fix my morality and ethics subroutines from when I was hacked eight years ago.

She logged the information and then let her fingers fly. Her eyes scanned everything as fast as she could. Access to the Smiths' old files, the visitors, the mechanics, the software developers and ship builders... The name imprinted on her mind, Torrent, never appeared anywhere.

Clicking out of the last file took her back to the main screen.

"I see you watching him. Best not to get any ideas." Snapper's deep timbre washed over her, a low rumble like when she'd be caught in the edge of a current floating through space and trying to get her bearings.

She froze. "What do you mean?"

"You watching Drag, getting that admiring look in your eyes like he invented Marsanium or something."

Turning slowly, Gina found little to no space between them. Two steps max, but they were eye-to-eye. The big difference between her and most of the other women in Frog Lick — they had to look up to him. Maybe she did intimidate him. Sampson had suggested as much on their last holo-call.

"He didn't invent Marsanium. The discovery was made by Jangles McKinney in 2292."

Snapper shook his head and muttered under his breath, "You're just a little walking encyclopedia and I know that, Gina. It was a comparison."

"A figurative method of speech? I'm afraid I don't see the reference clearly as I don't admire the invention of Marsanium, though I do admire Drag. He is a good leader." Hopefully, complimenting his best friend would deflect him away from noticing her inability to react to his figurative language. *Fatch.*

Snapper shook his head. "What are you working on here?"

"Just updating the maintenance records on the hauler and listing the parts and supplies I used." She crossed her arms behind her back and stood up as straight as possible, prepared to handle whatever attitude he responded with. She suspected more vitriol.

"A lot of open files to be logging basic information," he replied with a frown.

"I forgot where things were."

Snapper stepped closer. "Then allow me to show you again, though maybe you should spend less time reading books and memorizing facts about my planet and focus more on your job?"

Gina stood her ground. "I found everything, and I'll do better. See you at the meeting?"

She could smell his sweat, mixed with a citrusy flavor that reminded her of the lime grove on the planet

Eden. Sharp and bitter, much like him. Scents were another gift humans took for granted. She enjoyed the smell of new things, along with trying to determine which ones appealed to her.

This close she could also glimpse the hairs on his chin, as curly and wild as the ones on his head. Though they weren't all the same color though—dark brown, ginger, even a couple gray strands graced his face. Her exploration of his features meandered on to the Grecian nose, a near Roman-esque feature like the old books of Earth displayed. Bluest eyes with a smattering of wrinkles around the edges...and the indention between his brows that grew more pronounced every time he was frustrated.

"Gina, why are you looking at me like that?"

She reached into her back pocket and pulled out the towel there. Every mechanic kept one, though she didn't sweat like the others and rarely had a use for it. Now she reached up and rubbed the grease away from his temples, one by one.

He took in a sharp breath, almost a hiss. There a was creak and groan of metal at her side as he clenched his cyborg fist tight. Another difference... He, like Drag and a couple of the others, were enhanced with cybernetic parts. While she possessed more strength than the average human, there was a good chance Snapper could give back as good as she gave. *Another thing we have in common, but I can't tell him that.*

She froze, and slowly pulled her arm back. "There. Clean."

Her fingers still tingled from the limited contact with his skin. So much sensation, three thousand touch receptors in a fingertip. *How do you humans not go into overload from a fleeting touch?*

Snapper growled, that indentation between his brows back again. "Next time, Gina, ask for permission before you touch someone."

She dropped the cloth at his feet. "Excuse me?"

"Leave Drag alone too. He doesn't need you trying to moon after him."

"What does that mean? I don't moon after anything. You're implying the moon can move outside of its orbit?" She cocked her head to the side as he took a step back.

"And pick up that cloth."

He walked off without answering her question, on top of treating her like some Mars adolescent or a cleaning robot. She wasn't a damn robot anymore, and high time she showed him, too.

Home of Erotic Romance

Sign up for our newsletter and find out about all our romance book releases, eBook sales and promotions, sneak peeks and FREE romance books!

About the Author

Landra Graf consumes at least one book a day, and has always been a sucker for stories where true love conquers all. She believes in the power of the written word, and the joy such words can bring. In between spending time with her family and having book adventures, she writes romance with the goal of giving everyone, fictional or not, their own happily ever after.

Landra loves to hear from readers. You can find her contact information, website details and author profile page at https://www.totallybound.com